I was awakened by ⸺⸺⸺⸺⸺ smooth, steady ride on the highway. The car rocked as my dad drove into a small hotel parking lot. I knew it was late before I even asked my dad what time it was. The parking lot was eerily quiet, with only a few cars, and as I looked up to the drape-covered hotel windows, only one room had lights on. My dad and I walked under the glowing sign that read "Horizons Hotel" with the "z" and the "t" struggling to stay lit.

When my dad and I walked up to the front desk, I didn't know which was creepier, the dark and empty parking lot or the fact that no one was there to greet us. We stood there for at least a minute before we heard movement in the back and my dad yelled, "Hello. Is anyone there?"

We then heard a man gruffly respond with "Just a minute." We waited five minutes or more. It gave me a chance to look over the place I would call home for however long it took my dad to find us a place to live.

Suddenly, a door opened from behind the desk and I could hear a television. A man, tall like my dad, approached the desk. He was white, with close-cut hair, black peppered with gray, a thick moustache, and a beard along the sides of his face. He cleared his throat and apologized for keeping us waiting.

"No problem," my dad said and asked for a room with two beds. The man began opening drawers and shuffling papers, searching for things, as if it was his first day at his job and he had no training. He mumbled, "Where did she put it?" and "How does she know where anything is?" I could tell he was a smoker, not only from the smell of his clothes at his every move, but also from his yellowed teeth. It took a while, but the man managed to find a receipt for my dad's cash payment for one week and the keys to our room.

"I guess you can see I don't usually cover the desk," the man said.

"I did," my dad said, "but hey, it'll be our little secret."

Drifting

Lisa R. Nelson

Tiny Satchel Press
Philadelphia

Tiny Satchel Press
311 West Seymour Street
Philadelphia, PA 19144
tinysatchelpress@gmail.com
www.tinysatchelpress.com

Distributed by
Bella Books
P.O. Box 10543
Tallahassee, FL 32302
1-800-729-4992

Publisher/Art director: Maddy Gold
Editor-in-Chief: Victoria A. Brownworth
Cover design: Christopher Bauer
Cover production: Jennifer Mercer
Book design: Stacia Seaman
Tiny Satchel Press logo: Chris Angelucci

Printed in the United States of America.
First edition.
ISBN 978-0-9849146-0-9

This book is dedicated to you, Mom and Dad—wonderful parents whose unfaltering love and support has meant more to me than you'll ever know.

Chapter One

When my dad and I moved, I thought it was my fault. He didn't tell me it was, but he was upset for some reason. And when he's upset, he becomes very quiet. He didn't say much to me for several weeks. When *I'm* unhappy, I'm also silent and my dad jokes with me until I laugh, then he asks what is bothering me. His method works every time. But with him, I usually leave him alone until he's ready to talk again. Most times he'll tell me something, usually not to worry. This time, he wasn't even saying that. Plus, that move was unexpected.

People we've met say I look like my dad. I don't see it. Sure, we're both tall and have the same complexion, but I'm not like some kids who look exactly like their dads. We're both the color of hot chocolate with extra chocolate. But I think that's it. My eyes are round, his are more almond-shaped. My lips are fuller than his. We both have long legs and arms, but my dad has deep dimples when he smiles, and I don't. He wasn't smiling much. In fact, he hadn't done much talking, either. That's why I didn't even ask him if I could have scheduled a last hair appointment before we left. My hair reaches the tips of my earlobes and, because I don't visit the hair salon regularly, I just curl it at the ends. Luckily, I've learned how to use a hair dryer and curling iron to do my own hair. I would have asked my dad to make an appointment, but I didn't think I'd have gotten an answer. He was too silent.

I wished he would have talked to me. It could have been that he was too busy deciding what we were going to take and what we should have left behind. When we moved here, three years ago, I was eleven. *Here* was Richmond, Virginia, and we've lived here longer than anywhere else. I can remember us living in Michigan, a few months in Ohio and, the last place, Washington, D.C. We lived in a small apartment, then. It had no real kitchen, just a tiny space for a little table with a few cabinets lined across a wall above the stove, sink, and counter. There was one bedroom, which my dad let me have. He slept on the sofa bed and we shared the closet and dresser drawers that were in my room. We lived there for about a year, and then we moved to Richmond to an apartment with two bedrooms. I guess my dad figured that since I was getting older, walking in the living room and seeing him in his underwear, sometimes with a T-shirt, sometimes not, sprawled across a sofa bed and drooling on a pillow simply had to stop. I didn't particularly like seeing him like that myself. At least the Richmond place had a nice-sized living room and more space for a larger kitchen table for when my dad and I would sit together sometimes and have dinner. Most times he arrived home late at night. He worked with caterers to deliver food for parties, weddings, and meetings for business offices, and he would cover for other people who weren't able to make a delivery. So when he wasn't home, I would sit in front of the television and eat dinner. My dad cooks pretty well, so he'd prepare meals for us on the weekend and teach me at the same time, and all I'd have to do during the week was throw a dish in the microwave.

I'll miss some things about living in Richmond, and there are things I won't. Hopefully, my dad will get a new job with normal hours, so I won't be alone so much. He wouldn't let me have anybody over unless he was home. The only exception would be Ms. Baxter, who lived across the hall. I can say without any doubt or hesitation, I will not, absolutely will not, miss *her*. I think my dad always liked her because she told him everything I was doing. Once, I went outside to empty trash in the bin on the side of the building. I turned around, and there was Ms. Baxter in a stained flowered house dress, sweat socks halfway up her calves, and fluffy bedroom slippers. Her hair was in a just-as-busy flowered scarf, and she had a cigarette hanging out of the side of her mouth. She has bushy eyebrows, which she frowned over her squinting eyes. I jumped, not expecting anyone to be behind me, especially a sight like that.

"Whatchu doin'?" she asked me in her strong voice that sounded like a frog, if a frog could talk. I told her I was emptying trash. She looked behind and around me as if I was magically hiding someone. She acted like a suspicious detective who was really close to getting me to crack and confess to something, and wanted me to know it.

Ms. Baxter always did that to me and reported all of my actions to my dad. I would be in the living room and could hear her giving him all the details of whatever she thought she saw or heard. Before my dad even had a chance to put the key in the lock of our door, I would hear her open *her* door and say, "Darryl, I noticed Jasmine went downstairs to pick up a pizza at the front door. Did you let her order a pizza?"

My father would say, "Yes, Ms. Baxter, I did, and thanks." He had the nerve to thank her, a strange woman who had nothing better to do than spend her days and nights watching the less-than-thrilling life of a fourteen-year-old girl. It became so annoying that when my dad wasn't home, I just stayed inside, flicking the remote for hours or listening to music or making a phone call to the one real friend I had. I hate to say it, but somehow I think that's what my dad really wanted. He wanted me alone. But I didn't know why.

I was going to miss my friend, Rachel. She's tall, like me, but with a little more up top and on the bottom. I'm generally straight up and down, with tiny breasts and a rear end that I hope somehow becomes more fully developed. I was once called a bean pole by Nathan Carter, but I didn't really care. I glared at him and said, "Wow, we're in the same advanced class, but you could only come up with something that stupid."

Rachel swore that Nathan teased me because he liked me. At least that's what she said her mother always says is the gauge to see if a guy wants you to be his girlfriend. I didn't care about that, either. I didn't like Nathan at all. He spit when he talked and he stood too close to me, leaving me to deal with being sprayed and his less-than-fresh breath. I could never understand why he didn't know he had bad breath, especially since his nose is right above his mouth. And I don't know if I'll make another friend like Rachel. I would have lunch with only her, we would study together and, the few times my dad let me go anywhere without him, he allowed Rachel to join me. Still, my dad wasn't too fond of Rachel's parents. He thinks they ask too many questions, especially her father. Rachel said he's like that with everyone—in other words, her father is nosy.

But I didn't think we left because of Rachel's parents or because of anything I did at school. Besides, I'm usually quiet at school. Other than occasionally raising my hand in class and talking with Rachel, I'm not seen and not heard. Also, I wasn't in school. It was the summer, a few days after the July Fourth holiday. Actually, I thought we were leaving simply because I wanted to go to the movies. It was the opening day for a film I knew I wanted to see even before it was in the theaters. My dad and I were in line, not too far from the front door and, without us knowing, a newspaper photographer took some pictures of people waiting to enter. In the picture, you see my dad and me patiently waiting like everyone else. I didn't even know we were in the newspaper until Rachel showed it to me. I laughed about it. I rushed home to show my dad. He wasn't amused. In fact, he grabbed the paper from me and kept staring at it. He slowly sat down. I asked him what was wrong. He said "Nothing," slammed the paper down, and walked into his bedroom. That was the beginning of his silence. Then a few days later, he told me we were moving away.

"Away? Where?" I asked, almost screaming.

He told me Raleigh, North Carolina. I felt a lump in my throat as I began to cry and my stomach turned. *What about Rachel?* I thought. If I'm so far away, would we still be friends? And I was looking forward to having cute Mr. Anderson for math class in September.

My dad wouldn't give me a reason why we have to leave, except that it would be a new start. I told him I didn't want a new start, but it was no use. It was clear he had made his final decision.

So now I sat in the middle of the empty living room floor. Dad sold our furniture. He went outside to help two men load a van with our couch and the coffee table that I had picked out. I had seen Rachel the night before, and we hugged and promised to text each other all the time and call when we could. But my dad took my cell phone and I didn't know how long it would be before he'd give me another one. He said it would be easier to just buy me a new one with a new phone company once we settled in Raleigh. It was one more thing I didn't understand.

It was weird when Ms. Baxter hugged me. I felt her large breasts against my tiny ones and she squeezed me so tight that my sides ached. "I'm gonna miss you," she said, her froggy voice cracking. When she released me and I could breathe again, I looked at her watery eyes. She said, "You be a good girl," and went into her apartment.

"She really cares about you," my dad said.

How was I supposed to know that? It wasn't like she came over and asked me to play a game. I felt a little bad for Ms. Baxter. I wondered what she would do with her time after my dad and I left. Maybe she'd start watching the six-year-old boy who lived on the floor above us. If his parents were anything like my dad, they'd love it.

When we started on the highway in our 2002 Toyota, with bags piled high in the back seat and crammed in the trunk, I held back my tears. I didn't fully understand why it was all happening again.

I was born in Florida. My mother died when she had me. My dad told me the story of how her parents didn't want me and his parents weren't supportive. So he decided to leave Florida with me. He doesn't talk about his parents or my mother's family. My dad has one brother and he rarely speaks of him, either. So, it's just the two of us. I'm okay with it most times, and then there are other times, when I wonder if I'll ever meet my grandparents, my uncle, and my cousins, if I have any. Do they think of me and wonder where I am? Or am I a fleeting thought, like a leaf blown away by the wind?

"Are you all right, sweetheart?" my dad asked me. I could feel him throwing me quick glances as he watched the road. I consider my dad an intelligent man and I understood he wanted to express his concern, but seriously, how could he think I was anywhere near all right? I wasn't certain how to answer the question. Should I have lied and said I was fine? That's what I usually did to keep my dad from worrying about me. Or should I have been honest and told him why I thought we moved so abruptly? At first, I decided to simply shrug my shoulders.

"I know it might be hard for you to understand why we left."

"Was it my fault?" I asked. I wanted to know if we moved because of the picture in the newspaper.

"Oh, Jasmine," he said and grabbed my hand. "None of this is your fault. Don't ever think any of this is your fault."

"Then why did we have to leave?" I wanted my dad to be open and do more than make me feel good—I wanted the answer. My dad stared ahead, like he was trying to choose his words carefully. I'd seen that expression before.

He paused for a few seconds and said, "It was just time. But trust me, Jasmine, this is a really good decision for us. Can you try and understand that?"

I could. It was true. I trusted my dad with everything, no matter how confused I was sometimes. I knew he always wanted me to have the best, and I was aware of how hard he worked to get it. I didn't want him to be sad because *I* couldn't be mature enough to accept the move. I wasn't going to be a baby about it.

Although he said our drive wouldn't be too long, my dad and I stopped about two hours after we began our trip. After he filled up the gas tank and we both went to the restrooms, we stood in line at a fast-food restaurant.

"Jasmine?" a woman asked. I turned around. "Oh my goodness, it *is* you."

In front of me was Mrs. Warner, my science teacher from last year. I really wished Rachel could have been there to witness the very different Mrs. Warner. She had retired after I had her as my teacher. Rachel and I would create wild images of how our teachers were outside of the classroom. We envisioned Mrs. Warner living in an isolated house, cabin-like, with beakers, test tubes, and microscopes scattered in every room. She was a true science lover. She continuously reminded us to watch science programs and she gave us copies of magazine articles about science all the time. She used rhymes to help us remember formulas. Everyone thought we were a little too old for jingles, but I thought it was a cute attempt on her part to get us to understand the subject. And she always had a "don't do what I did" story, such as don't set half of your parent's kitchen on fire from mixing the wrong chemicals or don't dye a friend's hair because it may turn lime green and break off. There was no way *this* Mrs. Warner was who Rachel and I imagined—she was too stylish. Still a little flighty, like she was in class, but really stylish. She was with two other women her age, and all three were dressed in fashionable outfits even *I* would wear, from their earrings to their handbags. And Mrs. Warner had on make-up, with false eyelashes that were noticeable each time she blinked her blue eyes. Her sandy brown hair was down around her shoulders, with soft curls at the ends. *This* Mrs. Warner was so different from the one who stood in front of the classroom every day in baggy khakis and denim shirts that looked like she grabbed them from her husband's closet. I was happy to see Mrs. Warner and only hoped she didn't notice my surprise at how fabulous she looked. She had become my favorite teacher in junior high. I visited a science museum for the first time because of her. She understood that I liked animals. She was the only one besides my dad and Rachel who knew that I wanted to be a veterinarian. At my eighth-grade graduation, she pulled me aside to congratulate me and gave me a book on all types of animals, from ducks to orangutans.

"You've become so tall in one year," Mrs. Warner said.

I said hello to her and the other women and smiled at them. She greeted my dad and introduced the women as her friends, and then they went to wait for her outside.

"So what are you doing here?" she asked.

"My dad and I..."

Before I could tell her we were moving, my dad interrupted me and said that we were going to a family funeral in Connecticut.

"Oh, I'm sorry," she said. "Was it a close family member?"

"Thank you," my dad said. "It was my uncle."

Mrs. Warner nodded her head, said a few more kind things that adults say to each other when discussing the death of someone, and then asked me, "How do you like high school?"

I looked at my dad before I answered. He nodded his approval.

"I like it." That's all I said. I figured I should keep my answer short, not knowing how much I should say or *what* I should say.

"Good, good," she said. I wanted to tell her more. I wanted to tell her that I did well in school the past year, that Rachel and I were still good friends and, most importantly, that I was moving away.

My dad remained silent. I followed his lead and, because of our silence, I could tell Mrs. Warner was at a loss for words herself. Then she said, "Well, it was so

good to see both of you, especially you, Jasmine. Here."
She reached in her bag and wrote her phone number on
a piece of paper.

"Make sure you call me when you get back home. If
it's all right with your father, maybe we can have lunch
together."

"Thank you, Mrs. Warner," my dad said as he reached
for the paper. "I'll make sure Jasmine does."

Mrs. Warner looked at him strangely. My dad said
that he needed to keep the phone number because I
misplaced things sometimes. I struggled not to yell out,
"I *what*?" Actually, *I'm* the one who has to keep track of
where my father puts things.

"I understand that," Mrs. Warner said, "I had that
problem when I was her age, especially in my bedroom."
She laughed just as heartily as I remembered she did in
class at her own strange humor. And just like in class
with my classmates, I simply chuckled with my dad,
while she kept going as if she heard the funniest joke
from the funniest comedian. Mrs. Warner then hugged
me and said she'd look forward to hearing from me, and
then she walked away. When he thought I wasn't looking,
my dad balled up the paper and threw it away. When *he*
wasn't looking I ran back to the trash can and retrieved
the phone number. I couldn't believe he had done that. I
shoved the piece of paper in my pocket.

"Why couldn't we just tell Mrs. Warner we were
moving to Raleigh?" I asked my dad after we bought food
and walked to the car.

"Jasmine, you know how I am. You know I'm private
and don't like it when people ask too many personal
questions."

Now, *I* was looking at him strangely.

"And besides," he continued, "she would want to

know our new address and I'm not sure about all that yet, so instead I just told her we were going to Connecticut."

My dad sounded convincing, but something didn't seem right. Why did he toss Mrs. Warner's phone number? Maybe he thought it would be a waste of time to call her, since I wouldn't be able to have lunch with her anyway. He was right that we had no idea where we would live and that may have seemed odd to Mrs. Warner. It seemed odd to *me*. It would have been too much to explain to her. Besides, *I* wasn't even sure why we left.

Chapter Two

Hours later, we arrived in Raleigh. I was awakened by the car slowing down from the smooth, steady ride on the highway. The car rocked as my dad drove into a small hotel parking lot. I knew it was late before I even asked my dad what time it was. The parking lot was eerily quiet, with only a few cars, and as I looked up to the drape-covered hotel windows, only one room had lights on. My dad and I walked under the glowing sign that read "Horizons Hotel" with the "z" and the "t" struggling to stay lit. The lobby was bright, although I wished it wasn't. Dimmer bulbs in the old chandelier fixtures would have hidden the tears in the couch that was neatly placed opposite two wing chairs with an old rectangular wooden table in the center of the tiled floor. I supposed the owner wanted to give visitors a homey feeling to the lobby, but would have done a better job with newer furniture, cleaner drapes, and current magazines on the table, rather than ones advertising great Halloween ideas when it was early July.

When my dad and I walked up to the front desk, I didn't know which was creepier, the dark and empty parking lot or the fact that no one was there to greet us. We stood there for at least a minute before we heard movement in the back and my dad yelled, "Hello. Is anyone there?"

We then heard a man gruffly respond with "Just a minute." We waited five minutes or more. It gave me a chance to look over the place I would call home for however long it took my dad to find us a place to live. Hopefully, I thought, he would put more time into *that* search than he had for this choice of hotel.

Suddenly, a door opened from behind the desk and I could hear a television. A man, tall like my dad, approached the desk. He was white, with close-cut hair, black peppered with gray, a thick moustache, and a beard along the sides of his face. He cleared his throat and apologized for keeping us waiting.

"No problem," my dad said and asked for a room with two beds. The man began opening drawers and shuffling papers, searching for things, as if it was his first day at his job and he had no training. He mumbled, "Where did she put it?" and "How does she know where anything is?" I could tell he was a smoker, not only from the smell of his clothes at his every move, but also from his yellowed teeth. It took a while, but the man managed to find a receipt for my dad's cash payment for one week and the keys to our room. I wasn't surprised that my dad paid with cash or that the man didn't seem to mind, either. My dad didn't carry credit cards, but I knew he saved money. He had a small safe with a combination lock where he kept all the cash we had. I never knew how much was in there, but whenever there was something we needed, my dad would get just the right amount from the safe.

"I guess you can see I don't usually cover the desk," the man said.

"I did," my dad said, "but hey, it'll be our little secret."

The man chuckled and told us that in the morning

his daughter would be at the front desk. "Her name is Felicia," he said. "Just ask her for anything you need."

For the next hour, my dad and I unloaded the car and took everything to our room. The hallway on our floor was narrow with patterned carpeting, although it was so faded I could barely make out the design. The room was a simple space, covered wall-to-wall with dark brown carpet. There were two beds, a television on a long dresser, and a table with two chairs. I plopped down in a chair and looked at the room with our bags piled against a wall. I couldn't hide my disappointment. I missed home already. Everything we owned was stuffed in some duffle bags in a tiny room in a run-down hotel. "Why were we here?" I thought to myself.

My dad knelt in front of me. It was like he heard my thoughts. "I know this is hard for you, Jasmine." I wasn't sure if he knew how much. I would have given anything to be back in my own bed, knowing that I might be allowed to hang out with Rachel the next day, with a chance of running into schoolmates Marcus and the not as cute, but still good-looking Daniel around the neighborhood. This "situation" was only temporary my father told me. But I couldn't sleep that first night wondering what the "situation" was.

The next morning, I was awakened by my dad in the shower. The clock on the night stand read seven o'clock. The room was relatively bright from the sun, even though the drapes were still closed. When my dad came out dressed in his best pants, an undershirt, and barefoot, he told me he was going to start looking for a job.

"Already?" I asked hoarsely.

"There's no time to waste, baby girl. We need a place to live, don't we?"

"We already had a place to live," I mumbled.

My dad turned around. "And we'll get another one, Jasmine." I crossed my arms. He said, "You've got to try and understand..."

"Understand what, dad?" I interrupted.

"Understand that I know what I'm doing. Trust that I'm your father and I'm taking care of everything." My dad spoke slowly this time, and his tone—kind up to now—changed to one of impatience. But at that moment, I didn't care.

"Now, I want you to get dressed, so we can have breakfast," he said sternly and faced the mirror.

I jumped up angrily and did what I was told. That's how it's been with my dad and me. I'll keep asking questions and he'll try to get me to understand his point of view. Usually, I do. But sometimes I don't and he just shoots me down. That's how it was in Richmond whenever I insisted on knowing why I had to stay in our apartment when he wasn't home, or those times when I asked my dad too many questions about what he was like when he was my age. But for some reason this time was different. Leaving our home so quickly nagged at me.

We went to a diner for breakfast. In the booth, my dad gave me my only instruction. No surprises and very clear. I was to stay in the room at all times until he returned. He bought me snacks, a sandwich for lunch, a bottle of fruit juice, and a bottle of water. For the next few days, I did as I was told. I switched through television talk shows, reality shows, and music videos to see when Raleigh aired the same shows I watched in Richmond. At home, I was in front of the television for too many hours, there was no denying it. But it gave me company. Other than times with my dad or Rachel, that square box was my friend, but after awhile, even *it* couldn't keep me entertained in the hotel room, so I decided to go out.

Lisa R. Nelson

It was late morning when I stood at the hotel lobby window, staring at cars passing by on the main road. I took in the space alone before I met Felicia for the second time. The first time I had met her was when my dad and I went to the desk the morning after we got to the hotel. Felicia was there, flipping through a magazine. She then looked at us as if we had interrupted something really important, and she simply nodded when my dad asked if she was Felicia. Then she answered flatly when he asked where we could go for breakfast—she was almost rude. She had a fair complexion and I could tell she was biracial. Her hair, thick and wavy and pulled back in a pony tail, hung just below her shoulders. She had three earrings in each ear, a small hoop nose ring, and several rings on her fingers. After our exchange, she quickly returned to her reading. This time, as I stood in front of the window, she said to me, "I advise you to stay close. Your dad already asked me to keep an eye on you." I turned sharply and went to Felicia, partly because I couldn't believe what she'd said and partly because I was shocked that the lifeless figure behind the desk actually had a pulse and could say more than a few words at a time. I asked her to repeat herself. She said it again and added that my dad not only asked her to call him on his cell phone if I left the hotel during our stay, but he also gave her fifty dollars to do it.

"He what?" I asked sharply.

Felicia laughed at my surprise. "What did you do?" she asked me between snickers.

"Nothing," I snapped. I didn't like that the first time I saw her smile, let alone laugh, was at my expense. I started to walk away. She stopped laughing.

"Hey," she called.

I turned around as if to say, "Now what?"

"Just because your father asked me to call him doesn't mean I will." She smiled, a sneaky smile. "I have a father, too. I know what it's like."

And just like that, in one second, I went from hating Felicia to liking her.

For the next hour, I talked to Felicia at the front desk. She shared that she was nineteen and, like me, it was just her and her dad. Also like me, her mother had died, but Felicia was fifteen when she died. "Want to see a picture?"

I nodded. My mouth was full of the popcorn Felicia had made in a microwave in the back room. She showed me a family photograph of her when she was ten with her parents. The three of them sat one in front of the other, like they were sitting on leveled steps. Felicia's mother was a black woman, very close to the dark brown color of me and my dad. Her father was clean shaven in the picture, so I could really see how handsome he was. Felicia resembled her father more, but I could clearly see her mother's eyes in Felicia's eyes. Felicia talked about how she had loved working at the hotel after school with her mother. They always talked about new ideas, like decorating the lobby and rooms and how to impress visitors so they'd visit again. I looked around.

"Yeah, I know," she said. "You wouldn't know it now."

She was right about that. Felicia admitted she and her dad hadn't put as much care into the hotel since her mother died. Felicia's parents bought it when Felicia was five and, since she didn't have any brothers or sisters, she became the only other person who handled the family business. She said she still missed her mother. I could see she did by the way she kept staring at the photograph.

"So let me see a picture of your mother," Felicia said.

Her request came out of nowhere, as if she felt she had to snap herself out of thinking about her *own* mother.

"I don't have one," I told her.

"That's okay. Bring it down tomorrow so I can see her."

"No, I mean I don't have one at all."

Felicia frowned. "You mean your father didn't save at least one for you? You've never seen your mother?"

"Of course I've seen her, but we had a fire and all our pictures are gone."

"Wow, I'm sorry. That's a shame."

I looked hard at Felicia to see if she believed me.

"Well," she said, "all that matters is that *you* remember her up here," and she pointed to my head.

"Yeah, you're right," I responded and then told her I should go back to my room. I had started to feel uncomfortable and I didn't want her to notice it. As I walked away, I also felt weird. I had lied to Felicia as smoothly as my dad had lied to Mrs. Warner. It was too easy. It was true that I had seen my mother, but there was no fire, ever. The only picture I'd seen was one when my mother was about Felicia's age. She was standing in front of her house. She was smiling as wide as I did whenever my dad bought me something I really wanted for Christmas. She was tall and thin like me. She stood with her hand on her hip and her head tilted to the side. Felicia was on target. I did remember my mother in my mind, even though I saw the picture only a few times. My dad would take it and always said that he would keep it in a safe place because it was the only one we had of her. Until now, the story had worked. But after speaking with Felicia, it seemed strange to me that my dad wouldn't have more photos of the woman who was more than my mother—she was his girlfriend whom he said he loved. And why couldn't I see it anytime I wanted? Why did I have to ask him for it, followed by him asking why I wanted to see it? I sat on the bed filled with more questions, trying to get what was going on, and then I realized I had better eat my sandwich before my dad got back. I wouldn't want him to have any idea that I wasn't in the room the entire time he was away.

"You know, I was thinking," my dad began to say as he wiped his mouth with one of the diner napkins, napkins that felt like tissue paper. We were having dinner at the table in the hotel room. I had spaghetti with marinara sauce in a foam container. My dad had chicken parmesan. He had picked up the meals on his way home from another day of job searching. In the days we had been at the hotel, I had become tired of eating food either wrapped in foil or paper or placed neatly in take-out boxes. But we didn't have a choice. Once, Felicia shared leftovers with me, baked chicken and rice, from her dinner. She was a good cook, but because she was sharing her lunch, there was only enough for me to have a taste, which was actually a tease, as I craved more.

"So, what do you think?" my dad asked. I thought absolutely yes to his suggestion that we tour Raleigh during the upcoming weekend.

"It'll be good for you to get out of this room. I don't like you watching so much television."

It seemed okay to him when I was home, I thought. But I was glad my dad wanted us to do something together.

"I'll ask Felicia where she thinks we can go," I said, as I twirled my fork in the spaghetti.

"You know the front desk clerk well enough to ask her where we can go?"

Damn, I thought. I let myself slip in my excitement.

"I don't know her at all, Dad. I just remember her name." I lowered my eyes and kept eating. I knew my dad was staring suspiciously at me. I quickly added, "Besides, I thought I could plan our day with her help while you're out looking for a job."

"No!" my dad suddenly yelled. "You are to stay in this room when I'm not here. I thought I made that clear."

"But, Dad..."

"No, Jasmine. Just do what I said," he interrupted. He plunged his fork into his chicken. I knew he was angry with me again. I stared at him. He looked frustrated and wouldn't look up at me. "Listen, Jasmine, it's safer for you to stay in the room."

"Why is it safer? I just want to go to the lobby."

My dad took a deep breath and shifted in his seat. "You don't even know Felicia. We don't know anyone around here." My dad looked at my puzzled expression. His face turned softer. "I don't want anything to happen to you. I want to protect you."

"Just like at home?"

My dad said yes and smiled. It was then I realized that he and I were doing the same thing. He tried to fool me as I had just tried to fool him. He was keeping something from me. I could feel it. I just didn't know what it could be. So, I simply nodded my head as if to tell my dad I understood him. But what *he* didn't know was at that moment, I also felt afraid. *What was happening to my dad and me?* I had never lied to him, let alone anyone else, and I've never seen him so anxious or act so strangely. It seemed that as I got older, things became more complicated. Maybe my dad and I were like the sitcoms I would watch where the teenagers would have arguments with their parents for staying out too late or for getting in trouble at school. But I was always home and, until now, I followed my dad's every rule.

What was happening between us was very confusing. That night, my dad and I watched a movie. I pretended we were home in our Richmond apartment, laughing and talking like everything was normal. I had a feeling he was trying to do the same.

The very next day, I was back at the front desk with Felicia. I suppose I went out of spite, but mostly I went because I felt drawn to her like a kid to an ice cream truck on a summer day. When I first approached the desk, she was talking to a woman. Felicia seemed disinterested in what the woman was saying. As I reached them, Felicia looked pleased as if I was rescuing her from something. She introduced me to the woman, who was named Sabrina. She was a fair-skinned black woman with make-up so nicely done that she looked like she just walked away from the cosmetic counter at a department store. Her hair was in long, soft curls. She wore a tight, dark blue dress with very high-heeled shoes, large hoop earrings, a bracelet, and a small handbag over her shoulder. Her outfit looked like she was going out for the evening. This was not something to wear at ten in the morning. She was nice, though, and when she smiled, her whole face made her look even more pleasant. I could tell Sabrina was older that Felicia and me, probably in her mid-twenties. She told me it was nice meeting me and said, "Don't forget what I told you," to Felicia. Then she left the hotel. Felicia rolled her eyes.

"Looks like you don't like her too much," I said.

"She's a pain in the ass," Felicia responded.

"What's wrong with her? She seems nice."

"Don't let her kindness fool you," said Felicia, and then she changed the subject.

I told her about how my dad almost found out that I was spending time with her. She congratulated me for covering myself so quickly. I didn't feel proud. It bothered me that I was beginning to act as if I had something to hide. I found myself confessing to Felicia about my mother's picture. I told her there was no fire and that I hadn't actually looked at the photo for over a year.

"A year?" she exclaimed. "Why so long? Why don't you just have it in a frame next to your bed or something?"

I shrugged my shoulders and told her that my dad wanted to keep it in a safe place to protect it, since it's the only one we had. Felicia looked at me oddly.

"Nothing against your dad, but that sounds real strange." Before I could respond, the lobby door opened and a young mailman entered. Felicia's face lit up.

"Hi Ricky," she said.

"Hey, Lish," he said. He was *cute*. Ricky, brown like peanut butter, was muscular and a little taller than me, which meant he was about a foot taller than Felicia. For awhile they talked as if I wasn't there. And for the first time, I saw the usually cool and calm Felicia stumble over her words and nervously play with her hair.

Oh yeah, I thought to myself, *she's definitely crazy about this one.*

Ricky finally looked at me and said, "Hey, I'm Ricky. Who might you be?"

"I'm Jasmine."

"She's staying here with her father," Felicia said, only noticing my presence because Ricky had, and then they both returned to their discussion, forgetting about me. I decided I would leave them alone and go back to my room. I was bored when I got there, so I skipped through television channels. A little while later, there was a knock on the door. I looked through the peephole at Felicia and let her in.

"Why did you leave?" she asked me.

"Since you and your *boyfriend* were so into each other, I thought I would just come upstairs."

"Don't be like that," she said as she walked into the room. She admired how neat my dad and I kept things. "Even *my* bedroom isn't this clean."

I asked Felicia where she lived. She said she and her dad had an apartment at the back of the hotel, so that they could keep an eye on things. "You wouldn't believe how nasty some people can be in this place."

She plopped on the edge of my bed and I asked her who was at the front desk. She told me Sabrina. "She covers sometimes when I need a break."

I sat down next to Felicia and asked her questions about Sabrina and Ricky. Felicia was evasive, but I managed to learn that Sabrina watched over her like Ms. Baxter had with me and that Felicia was just as annoyed by it as I was. Sabrina was exactly thirty and Felicia's dad had known her from the neighborhood where he grew up.

"She knew my mother too, but my mother wasn't very fond of Sabrina."

"Why?" I asked, eager to know as much as I could about Felicia and her family.

"She just wasn't." Felicia was vague again, so I shifted gears to focus on Ricky. Her face brightened at the mention of his name, but she tried unsuccessfully to brush off his importance to her. "He's just our mailman and a friend of mine."

"Yeah, I bet."

Felicia stood up and now turned the conversation to me. "You and your father sure didn't bring a lot of stuff."

I was silent.

"Y'all know anybody here in Raleigh?"

I shook my head.

She walked and looked around the room like a detective, searching under menus on the table, peeking over the trash can. I wasn't worried. My dad kept everything private from me. There was no way Felicia would find anything that he wouldn't want to be found.

"How did you and your father end up here?"

I shrugged my shoulders. I began to feel I was being interrogated for a crime well beyond the few lies I told.

"Maybe your father knows somebody in Raleigh who you don't know. Isn't that a possibility?"

I remained frozen. I was uncomfortable, but I didn't want Felicia to leave. Even with all her questions, I still wanted to be close to her. Besides, *she* didn't make me uneasy—the fact that I couldn't answer her questions did. She finally looked at me and apologized for making me nervous. It must have shown all over my face.

"No, it's okay. I kinda wondered myself why my dad decided that we move here." I had asked my dad that question and he said he'd visited the city with his brother and parents when he was young and always remembered it fondly. When I told Felicia, she seemed excited.

"Well, did he say who they visited? Did you ever ask your grandparents or your uncle why they came here?" I shook my head and Felicia said, "That's it. There's your answer. You can call them downstairs and your dad will never know you made a long distance call. C'mon." She jumped up and went to the door. I sat still.

"What's wrong?" she asked.

I felt like I was in a television movie at the point when the music begins, right before a commercial break, leaving viewers to wonder how much the character would reveal.

"Can I trust you, Felicia?" It may have been an odd question to ask someone I had known for less than a week, but honestly, I felt I *could* trust her.

"Of course, girl, what's wrong?"

I explained what my dad told me about his family.

"So you never met any of them?"

I looked down and said no.

"Do you know where they live?"

I mumbled Florida, adding that they didn't want to have anything to do with my dad and me. Felicia was empathetic. She put her arm around me. I could have cried right then, but she said something I had not considered.

"Why don't you look for them anyway?"

"What if they still don't want to know us?"

"But what if they do and they don't know where you are?" Felicia assured me she would help me search for not only my dad's side of the family, but my mother's as well. She even gave me an assignment. I was to write down everything I remembered that my dad had told me about everybody—names, locations, *everything*. Now *I* was excited. When she left the room, I sat down, writing. The trouble was that I was soon looking at a blank piece of paper. In fact, after I wrote my father's name, Darryl Hinton, born in Florida, on August 29, 1977, there was nothing more to remember. With nothing else to add, I balled up the paper and threw it in the trash can.

"Dad, after we get settled, can we go to Florida?" I shouted the question to him while he brushed his hair in the bathroom. It was Saturday, the day of our Raleigh tour. As I had expected, my dad went to Felicia alone to find sight-seeing locations.

"Why?" he asked, as he walked into the room.

"Well, I was thinking, if that's where my grandparents and uncle are, maybe we could go find them?" I actually thought *this* time my dad would finally have a change of heart.

He exhaled. "Jasmine, we went over this before. I left on bad terms with them. They didn't support you or me. I don't want to have anything to do with them."

"But maybe things changed. Maybe they want to see you again."

"Where is all this coming from?"

I told him that being away from home made me want to be with family, especially being alone in the room all day. *Boy,* I thought to myself, *If Felicia was proud of me before, she should hear me now*. My dad melted like butter in a hot pan, comforting me, but not enough to agree to search for our family. I even tried to find out what city my dad was from, but he said it wasn't important. So, I made my decision out of frustration. Felicia and I would find my family without him, even though I had almost nothing with which to begin the search.

Chapter Three

Dad and I had so much fun in Raleigh—it was like being on a rollercoaster. I loved my dad like this. And on a summer Saturday afternoon, we definitely weren't the only people who thought touring the city would be a great idea. I wasn't complaining, although I thought I would scream if another person bumped into me while my dad and I stretched our necks or crouched down to look at a museum exhibit. I was just glad to see my dad more relaxed than I had seen him in a long while. It was a really good time, until we saw the little girl. We were in the park and had just inhaled hot dogs smothered in mustard, ketchup, and sauerkraut. A woman blew bubbles and a little girl, who looked about two years old, in pigtails and a summer dress, jumped up and down and laughed hysterically as she tried to catch the bubbles. She *did* look cute, but my dad couldn't keep his eyes off her. After a little while, I was over the little girl, but my dad never looked away. Then he said, "I remember when I used to do that with you. And you did just what she's doing."

I looked at her again, and back at my dad, and didn't understand what was so thrilling about her doing the same thing over and over. It was like he was mesmerized by her. He actually began to tear up.

"Dad," I said sharply, which snapped him out of his trance. "What's wrong?"

He laughed it off, quickly wiped his eyes, and told me that nothing was wrong. "Sometimes I miss those times when you were little. You're so big now."

Finally, the mother and the little girl walked away and I watched my dad watch them disappear through the bike riders and the crowds of people that strolled past us. He turned to me, smiled, and told me he was proud of me. He put his arm around me and kissed me on the top of my head. Then we left the park to head back to the hotel. It was a solemn trip back. The closer we got to the hotel, the more my dad's mood shifted to where it had been before we left that morning. I had to admit, I wasn't all that eager to return. When we entered the lobby, Sabrina was in one of the chairs, flipping through magazine pages. She was in a red dress this time, with a different pair of high-heeled shoes.

"Hi, Darryl. Hi, Jasmine," she said to us. My dad and I looked at each other—I didn't know he knew Sabrina, and he didn't know that I knew her as well. We each said hello and kept walking. Felicia's eyes were big and she mouthed to me, out of my dad's view, "I'm sorry," and I knew she had forgotten to give Sabrina a warning.

"So you *have* been leaving the room!" My dad could hardly wait to close the door before he charged at me. I was confused again. Didn't he just tell me less than an hour ago that he was proud of me? We'd had a good day, and now he was out of control. I couldn't even squeeze in my routine question of why I *had* to stay in the room. But he was more than just yelling—he seemed frantic. I just sat still and watched him pace the floor. He was literally out of breath when he stopped his rampage. He plopped in the chair.

"Jasmine, you've got to listen to me when I tell you to do something."

I didn't say anything. He told me he knew it was hard for me to be in the room all day. How would he know that?

"That's why we eat out sometimes, why I took you out today, and why we'll go out again soon," he said. He was calmer, so I simply apologized and lied that I met Sabrina the one time that I left the room. I figured I'd tell Felicia later to warn Sabrina to keep up the story. I told my dad that I kept it from him because I knew that he would be very upset. I even threw him a heavy dose of sadness all over my face. I wouldn't say my dad recovered quickly. He was very angry, but somehow I came away from everything without a punishment, although I thought to myself, *what would be the penalty, stay confined to my room?* He repeated how important it was to follow his rules. He said he didn't want to have to call every hour to check on me, but he would if I didn't "change my behavior." So, for the next few days I stayed in the room and my dad called several times, so by day four of our second week at the hotel, he went down to two calls, and by day five, he didn't call at all. By the time I returned to the front desk, I felt like I hadn't seen Felicia in months.

"Damn, girl, if I didn't see your father every day, I would have thought you left," Felicia said.

"Yeah, well, if *someone* had let Sabrina know what was going on, maybe *someone* would have seen me before now."

Felicia apologized again and assured me that Sabrina would keep quiet. I missed Felicia. I wished Rachel could meet her. I knew they would like each other.

"How can you be sure Sabrina won't say anything?" I asked Felicia. I sat on a stool, in my usual spot behind the desk and next to her.

Lisa R. Nelson

"Trust me, I'm sure." Felicia was reviewing some receipts in a book.

"You don't have a lot of people stay here, do you?" Since I began making trips to the lobby I had only seen a few people stop in. Two were a couple—he was in a suit with streaks of gray hair though his light brown hair, and she was a blonde, also in a suit, but didn't look much older than Felicia. They came together every other day around the same time and only stayed for an hour. I knew why they were there and Felicia had to know, but she didn't seem to care. It was routine. She checked them in each time like they were new customers. Felicia asked his name, since he paid for the room. The blonde would wait by the lobby window. Felicia would give him a receipt, the keys, and the room number. She didn't smile at him—in fact, she barely looked at him. And then the two would walk arm-in-arm, giggling.

"We have our busy times and our slow times," Felicia said, still calculating receipts.

"When are the busy times?" I hadn't seen any.

"I don't know. They vary," she snapped.

Just then, Sabrina walked in, escorted by a man around her age. He was white, with dark hair. He reminded me of the Italian actors I had seen on television. He had on a construction uniform and he looked *very* happy. Sabrina spoke to us and jokingly sang to me, "I don't see you!" and she winked.

I laughed and told her thanks. Felicia didn't see the humor.

In fact, when Sabrina said, "Give me the key to room 105," Felicia reached in the drawer and handed Sabrina the key without looking up. I sat silently while Sabrina and the man walked away.

"Now do you see why I don't care for her?" Felicia

rose and went in the back office to get something. It had to be upsetting. As much as Ms. Baxter irked me, I couldn't have imagined her as a prostitute. For one thing, I don't think many men would find her bulky bathrobe and the fluffy slippers very sexy. I *did* have a problem with Sabrina sleeping with men for money, so I could only imagine what it did to Felicia. I wanted to say something to give Felicia another point of view. But what could it be?

When Felicia returned, I asked her how Sabrina became close to her and her dad. After her mother died, Felicia said, Sabrina would visit the hotel regularly, "but not with customers." Sabrina simply visited to check on Felicia and her dad. She even prepared meals for them.

"Then all of a sudden," Felicia said, "she started looking after me, like I was her child, wanting to check my homework, asking me about my high-school graduation and college. My father loved it. It was like I had a mother again. But she's not my mother. My mother wouldn't sell her body."

"But it's good that she wants to care for you." Felicia didn't answer. She went back to her work. I sat quietly for a minute before I said to her, "Can I ask you something?" She looked at me. "My dad knows Sabrina. Does he... Did she... Do you know if..."

"They just talked a few times," Felicia said.

"Where?" I asked.

"Right here, in the lobby."

"Are you sure?"

Felicia nodded. I tried to let myself believe her. I remembered the few times at home when my dad would come home late, and not because he was working. I now wondered if he was with women like Sabrina. Did he want to be with *her?*

Lisa R. Nelson

"If he does, you shouldn't worry about it. I mean, your dad *is* a man."

I didn't like the sound of that. I wanted my dad to have a girlfriend, a wife even. Just sex with a prostitute, even if it was Sabrina, who I liked... I squirmed in my seat.

"Hey, don't get all bothered about it."

I couldn't hide my discomfort from Felicia.

"If I see anything suspicious, I'll let you know."

I stared at her, searching for confirmation that I could trust that she would, but I had a feeling that if she *did* see something, she might keep it to herself to protect me.

"So," she said. "Where's your list?"

I could tell Felicia changed the subject for me. I told her there wasn't a list and the reason why.

"That's all you know?" she asked.

I was embarrassed. I had no pictures, no family names, not even a city where my dad grew up. Felicia was surprised, but that didn't stop her.

"Well, there's no better time than now to see what we can find. C'mon." She took me into the office, to the back room that I had never seen. It wasn't very special. A microwave with a knob was on a small rickety table in a corner. An old white table was up against a wall with a computer keyboard and monitor in the middle it, a large hard drive on the floor under it. Loose papers, large and small, were scattered on the table, along with sealed envelopes that looked like bills and other important documents. Felicia turned on the computer. It took a while for it to warm up, and the Internet service took just as long. I had a laptop computer at home, but my dad didn't let me have Internet access. I used the Internet at school, the library, or sometimes at Rachel's house.

I don't have the laptop anymore. My dad sold it right before we left Richmond.

Felicia began moving the mouse around on a worn mouse pad and clicking the keyboard to reach a search engine. She worked as if I wasn't there. She typed all sorts of words in the search box—my dad's name, Florida, and different cities in Florida. Sure, my dad's name appeared, but the list of names included people who weren't him or their names were spelled differently. Felicia didn't appear frustrated as she tried to find a clue to track down my family. Nothing seemed to work. We were at it for two hours. The only thing that kept me calm was that Felicia was calm, until she noticed something on the desk. While we waited again for the slow computer to display another search list, Felicia looked over a batch of envelopes. She pulled one from under several others and said aloud, "What is this?"

I tried to decipher what it said but I couldn't. "What's the matter?"

She silently handed me the envelope. I was shocked. Felicia could be so contradictory—sometimes she trusted me, and other times she was evasive. This was a trusting time. The envelope was addressed to her dad with the hotel's address. The return address had a logo for a real estate firm. I didn't understand, so I asked her what it meant.

"Don't you get it?" she asked, sounding frustrated. I shook my head, feeling dumb.

"Obviously, my father is talking to somebody about selling this place, and he didn't want me to know."

"Oh," I said and felt afraid for her. I'd just left *my* home, so I knew how worried Felicia was. After that, she wasn't in any mood to continue searching online for my family, which was just fine. We had no luck in finding my family—it seemed a lost cause. I wondered if maybe my dad's parents and his brother had moved away. Maybe my dad was right—maybe they didn't want to have anything to do with us. I wondered if my dad's approach was best—just forget about them. As I sat thinking over that dreadful possibility and Felicia was in silence over her own shock, the office door opened. Her dad entered. I stood quickly, afraid of him seeing me sitting with his daughter at the computer.

Felicia grabbed my arm and pulled me back into the seat. She whispered, "I'll make sure he doesn't tell your father anything." It probably wouldn't have mattered. Felicia's dad moved around the room, ignoring me. I hadn't seen him since my dad and I first checked in. This time, he was shaven, as he had been in the photo Felicia showed me. He had on a black blazer with khaki pants, a white shirt, and a striped tie. He had a folder in his hand and he went straight to the desk. He grabbed a pen and some of the envelopes, including the one we had seen.

"I'm going to a meeting. I'll be back." He seemed distracted.

"What kind of meeting?" Felicia asked.

"Just some basic stuff. Nothing to worry about."

I've heard that before, I thought to myself. Felicia's dad kissed her on the top of her head and walked out. She jumped up, followed him, and closed the door behind her. I could hear them talking softly. Actually, Felicia sounded like me when I pleaded with my dad for answers. And just like my dad, hers kept his calming tone, probably trying to reassure her. After a few minutes, she returned and plopped down in the chair. I know the feeling of dissatisfaction, which I read all over her face. I kept quiet and waited for her to speak first.

"I've got to find out what this is all about."

"How?" I asked her.

"I don't know yet, but I will."

And that was it. Felicia shut down the computer, and we agreed to meet again the next day. She apologized for not being able to find anything. I told her it wasn't her fault, and then I asked her if she was okay. She admitted the thought of moving made her nervous. I told her that I understood.

"I mean, where does he want us to move?" she asked as we went back to the lobby.

"Do you ever think about going to college?" I asked.

"I used to. But I can't go now. My dad needs me." She said she would study business management if she could go to college, because she liked managing the hotel. "I know it doesn't look like much, but this place is my home." She looked around the lobby and continued to tell me that the hotel hadn't been doing well in a while. I couldn't have faked a surprised expression if I'd wanted to. Even Sabrina gave Felicia's dad a portion of the money she made to help keep the hotel in operation.

"Anyway," Felicia said, "my mother wouldn't like it if I left my father to care for this place by himself."

I wanted to keep talking to Felicia. I wanted her to keep sharing with me, but I knew my dad would be back soon. On my way to the room, I thought about college myself. I still wanted to be a veterinarian. Would my dad let me go when it was time? Would we have the money? I stretched out on the bed, thinking about things I hadn't thought of before. I knew I would have to start school again after my dad found a job. What was that going to be like? I dozed off, and was awakened by my dad gently shaking me.

My dad had found a job. He was in a good mood, so we went out for dinner. "Now, don't make fun of me for having to wear a company shirt," he said about his job at a car rental office. I made myself laugh. I was happy for him, but my mind was also on something else.

"You're really quiet. Is everything okay?" he asked as I picked through the strips of chicken tenders I'd ordered. I shrugged my shoulders. He said what he'd said many times before, that I could tell him anything.

"Will I be able to go to college?" I asked.

"Of course, Jasmine, if that's what you want to do." He responded right away, like I'd asked him if I could watch television when we went back to the room.

"What if I want to go away?"

He exhaled. I was making him uncomfortable again. He clenched his jaw. "Like where?" he asked, without looking at me.

"I don't know yet. But would you let me go?"

"It depends on where."

I asked him what he meant by that. He became agitated and quickly told me we would discuss it when the time came. I didn't push it.

"Hey," my dad said with a smile. "When we get back, why don't we play a game of cards?"

It wasn't that easy any more. My dad, trying to make me smile with games and funny faces to make me feel better, was middle-school stuff. I didn't want to play a game. I didn't feel up to playing cards. He tried to persuade me, but I still told him no. He looked puzzled, but stopped asking. We ate the rest of our dinner in silence, the way our meals had been lately. My dad would try to talk, but what was there for me to talk about? I couldn't tell him that I had found a new friend in Felicia, and I knew that too many questions about him would lead nowhere.

For the first few days at the hotel, my dad and I took

time for breakfast at a nearby diner. Now, we resorted to grabbing something quickly, like muffins or cereal. He said it would save time and money, but I suspected he thought, *why should we pay to sit in silence?* I ate my meals in the room, except lunch, which I had with Felicia. And by the end of the second week, I struggled to find something to talk about when we ate dinner. It felt like it was a challenge for him too. Things had changed between us, and I was worried.

Chapter Four

Saturday morning, two days before my dad's first day of work, I gathered our clothes to take to the laundromat after my dad picked us up something quick for breakfast. As I separated the colors from the whites, I felt myself becoming increasingly upset. I started to cry and couldn't stop. Nothing made sense to me—our abrupt leaving, how different things had become, how increasingly anxious my dad was. I quickly threw water on my face, because if my dad saw me like this, he would want to comfort me, and I knew he couldn't. I didn't want my dad to know how I was feeling. I didn't want to hear him say the same things he always said. I really wanted to talk to Felicia, but my dad said he wouldn't be long.

At the laundromat, my dad was engrossed in the sports section of the local newspaper. I sat next to him and switched my attention from our clothes rotating in the dryers to the activities of the other people who were waiting for their clothes to finish. One was absorbed in his cell phone, and another bobbed her head to the music on her iPod. Some people talked and folded clothes, and a few others read magazines or watched the laundromat television. But there was one woman, around Sabrina's age and close to her complexion, who paid little attention to her two young kids, who swung on carts. Instead, she yelled at someone on her phone. "Don't be so naïve," the woman said impatiently. She snapped her fingers and signaled to the children to take the clothes from their dryer. "She's lying to you," the woman said. She was silent for a few seconds and listened to the person on the other end. Then the woman said, "She has too many secrets and anyone with that many secrets can't be trusted."

That's it, I thought to myself. For the first time, I didn't trust my dad, and it scared me. Sure, I could count on him to protect me and to take care of me. But he was keeping something from me, and whatever it was, it also kept him from trusting me. I looked at my dad like I didn't know him. He glanced at me and smiled, but it quickly faded. I think he was confused by the way I looked at him. I couldn't hide my expression. I didn't even try. He started to say something, but our dryer stopped spinning. He got up and gathered the clothes. I watched him.

I needed to talk to Felicia. That night, while my dad slept, I wrote. I listed Ms. Baxter watching me, how I had to stay at home all the time, and not only the lie my dad told Mrs. Warner, but that he threw away her phone number. The next morning, right after my dad left for work, I showed the list to Felicia.

"So what does this mean?" she asked me.

"I don't know. That's the point."

She looked at me strangely and then went back to the list. "Maybe your dad is just very, very private, like he said."

I reminded her that he paid her money to look after me when he had just met her.

"Okay," she said, "maybe your dad's in some kind of trouble. Maybe he did something criminal, like stole some money or killed somebody, and you're on the run with him."

"Killed somebody! My dad is too nice to do that."

Felicia laughed heartily and, when she came up for air, she said, "Listen, a criminal can be as nice as a little old lady in a church choir. Kindness has nothing to do with it. And besides, you're his daughter. He wouldn't show his true colors in front of you."

I shook my head. No way was my father running from the law. He couldn't be. *Or could he?* But what type of crime could he have committed? Could he have stolen something—or worse?

"What do we do now?" I asked. Now I felt scared. I almost wished I hadn't brought it all up.

"I'm not sure," Felicia said, her voice strange.

Later, while I was in the room alone, I watched a crime show. I studied the criminal in the program and how he tried to get away with what he did. He didn't. By the time my dad came into the room, I was sure he was nothing like the character I had seen. I didn't care what Felicia said. My dad was too private and he had been acting way too strangely, but there was no way he was anything like the guy on the TV show.

"Here," Dad said, when he came in. He gave me a plastic bag filled with books. He turned off the television. "Like I said before, you're watching too much TV, so I got you some books to read."

As I pulled each one out of the bag, he gave me his explanation or why he bought it. He told me he got me a math workbook and an English grammar since I would be going back to school in about a month. And he got me *Black Boy* and *Catcher in the Rye* because he had to read them in high school.

"Why not get a jump start on it? They still read those classics," my dad said. "I'm serious, Jasmine. I want you to spend less time in front of that television."

I told him okay, but I wasn't all that happy about it.

I knew my dad. He'd definitely check the books to make sure the pages had been turned and he'd probably want to know what I thought of the stories. How was I supposed to read and spend time with Felicia?

The next day, I ran to the lobby to see her when my dad left for work. She was talking to Ricky. I stayed back and leaned against the wall. Maybe I shouldn't have eavesdropped, but I did. Felicia asked Ricky why not. He said because she was too young. She told him only in age, but that she was very mature. He chuckled and said he was sure of that. She asked, so what's the problem? He told her there was no problem, but he didn't want her dad to leave him needing a neck brace, crutches, and massive dental work. They laughed together. Then she asked Ricky if he knew anything about important mail addressed to her dad.

"Like what?" he asked.

"Like something from a realtor?" He must have looked at her questioningly, because she said, "C'mon, Ricky. I really need to know."

"What do you need to know?" he asked. She looked away, and then he said. "Tell me the truth. What do you need to know?"

"Is he trying to sell the hotel?"

"All right. Just don't say anything, but yes, I think your father wants to sell the hotel."

A shock wave ran through me, almost as strong as I knew it would be running through Felicia.

"That's bullshit!" she yelled. "He wouldn't do that without talking to me first."

I kept very still. I really didn't want her to know I was there.

"Hey, you asked what I thought." Ricky sounded defensive.

"What makes you say that?" Felicia asked. She sounded so sad.

Ricky replied that letters from realtors had been arriving for awhile. He also noticed that her father and Sabrina were having secret conversations in the parking lot.

"So, that doesn't mean he's selling the hotel," Felicia said.

Ricky described an incident that happened before my dad and I arrived. While Felicia was out and Ricky was taking mail out of his truck, he noticed her dad giving a man a tour of the outside of the hotel. "I watched your father point out different places and the man kept writing things down. And that wasn't the first time I had seen him, either."

"Why didn't you tell me all of this?" Felicia's voice cracked.

"I don't know, Lish. I guess I figured your father would take care of it." There was silence, then Ricky said, "Aww, Lish, don't get yourself so upset. It's all going to work out."

"How?" I could hear her crying. Ricky tried to console her as much as he could, but nothing seemed to work, and besides, he was still on duty. He stayed a little longer and promised that he would call her later.

I couldn't leave her there alone, but I waited about a minute so it would seem that I had just walked down to see her. I pretended I didn't know anything, but no one could ignore that her face and eyes were red. She wiped her face quickly when she saw me. I said hello and immediately asked her if she was okay.

"It's nothing." She was abrupt.

"Are you sure?"

"Yeah. Listen, Jasmine, can we talk some other time? I have some things to finish up."

She barely looked at me. I nodded and walked away. I wanted Felicia to talk to me. I felt that I was the only one who really understood how angry and hurt she must have been. Secrets were kept from me too. I couldn't imagine that her dad would keep something so important from her—he seemed so normal. But then, so did my dad. They were alike in that way, and they were alike in hiding things from us. I knew they loved us, but they'd made it hard for Felicia and me to trust them. So, I knew how Felicia felt. She was just like me. She might pretend that everything was okay, just like I had lately with my dad. And even if she confronted her dad with everything, she knew he would probably give her more stories, like my dad had with me. I didn't want to return to the room. I didn't want to act excited like my dad had ever since he had found a job. My stomach turned as I walked down the hallway. Soon we would be leaving. It was weird, but leaving the hotel was like moving away from home again, moving away from a friend again. Would I see Felicia once her dad sold the hotel? Would I lose her, like I had I lost Rachel? How could I feel happy like my dad, who was happy not only because he had a job, but also because he was probably close to saving enough money for us to move? Lately, he had been talking a lot about us being in our own home.

Chapter Five

I didn't see Felicia for a couple of days. I had nothing to do but read and work on math and English problems. My dad made good selections with the stories, which I enjoyed. In between studying those, I would venture into the lobby. Felicia's dad was always there. He said Felicia wasn't feeling well and was in bed. I was worried about her. A week ago, Felicia had given me her cell phone number. We both knew that I wouldn't be able to use it in the evenings, but she wanted me to have it so I could keep in touch whenever my dad wasn't in the room. I called it each day, and each time, I heard her message, "Hey, I'm not available, so you know what to do." I left messages that I was thinking of her.

Finally, after a few days, in the late afternoon, she was at the desk. I was so happy to see her. She was in a dress, her hair was out and curly all over, and she had on some make-up. I didn't know what to ask her first, how she was or why was she dressed up?

"Hi, Felicia, are you okay? Your dad said you weren't feeling well."

"Hey, Jasmine." She looked just as happy to see me. "I'm fine. I just told my father that."

"You sure look fine. You look pretty."

"Can you keep a secret?" she asked me. I was ready. I had been thinking about the sale of the hotel so much,

I was prepared to encourage her. I told her of course I could keep her secret.

"I invited Ricky over to see me when he gets off from his shift. I straightened up one of the rooms just for us." I was confused. What was she talking about?

"What do you mean? Why?"

"What do *you* mean, why? You know..." Felicia and I talked about almost everything, but we only discussed sex in reference to Sabrina.

"Did he say he was coming over?"

"Yes, but he doesn't know why. I told him I really need to talk to him."

"Have you ever done this before, Felicia?" After I said the words, I realized that maybe I had asked something a little too personal, but she didn't seem to mind.

"Yeah, my first time was a few years ago, when I was sixteen. It was with my boyfriend from school." As she talked, she kept looking at herself in the mirror, putting on lipstick and spreading her pinky finger around the edge of her lips. "Ricky should be here soon."

"Is that your secret?"

"Yeah, why?"

I shook my head. "Are you sure you want to do this? I mean, you and Ricky aren't dating or anything."

"Trust me, I'm sure." She was determined. It was all strange. Felicia seemed strange. Just then, Ricky walked in. He spoke to both of us, and Felicia looked at me like she was telling me to leave, which I did. I thought about her all night. Morning seemed like it would never arrive. I was anxious and couldn't wait to see Felicia.

She held a tissue in her hand and had a blank look on her face. Her hair was again in a pony tail. She acted like she was busy but, as usual, there were no customers.

"Well, how did it go?" I asked.

"All right." She went into the office, pretending to be busy. You would have thought there was a row of impatient people waiting to be checked in. When she returned, I asked her what happened the night before.

"Not much."

This time I couldn't stand her silence. This time I wouldn't let her get away with it.

"Damn it, Felicia!" I yelled. "Tell me what's going on with you!"

She broke down. She cried like I had the day I was sorting laundry. I went behind the desk and put my arm around her and just listened.

Felicia *had* asked Ricky to join her in the room. He asked her why she was dressed so nicely. She told him not to worry about that and added she had something to show him. He followed her into the room that she selected especially for them. She had candles lit on the tables and some flowers on the bed.

"I had the room so nice for us," Felicia said, wiping her nose.

Ricky had asked her, "What's all this?" She told him it was for them. She confessed to him that she had always liked him and whispered in his ear that she suspected he liked her too.

"I took his hand and pulled him to me and kissed him on his neck, then on the cheek, and then I sat on the bed."

"What did he do?" I asked anxiously.

Felicia paused and looked down. "Not a thing. He said, 'C'mon, Felicia, we can't do this,' and I said, 'Sure we can.'" Felicia took off her shoes and began to undress when Ricky yelled, "Felicia, stop!" He knelt down at the edge of the bed and told her that it was nice she cared about him and that he cared about her, but not in that way.

I knew what "that way" meant.

"I begged him to stay with me," Felicia said and started crying again. I was sad for her. "He held my hands and stood me up and then he hugged me. I didn't mean to, but I started to cry. I was so embarrassed."

"What happened then?" I asked.

"We sat and talked."

"About how you feel about him?" Felicia shook her head. They talked about the hotel. Felicia finally confided in me.

"I can't believe my father's doing this. I haven't even talked to him about it."

"Why did you call Ricky?"

"I don't know. I guess I thought he would help me feel better."

"Did he?"

"Yeah, but not in the way I thought he would."

Felicia talked about her mother. "Just because my father is selling the hotel, that doesn't mean I'm going to forget about mother."

I wondered if that's what Felicia's dad wanted her to do. Is that what my dad wanted me to do all along?

"He can't make me forget her," she said.

"Mine, neither," I said. Felicia suspected her mother would never want to sell the hotel. So, naturally, she wondered how her dad could do it.

"Maybe you should ask him." I couldn't believe I even suggested that. But maybe her dad was different than mine and would tell her the truth.

"I'm not asking him anything. He didn't think about me when he made his decision. He didn't even care about me or my mother." Felicia's eyes filled with tears again. "I wish she was here," she said, her voice quivering. "She'd know what to do."

Just then, Sabrina walked in. She wasn't in her working clothes—she had on jeans and sneakers. She was carrying bags full of groceries. She walked up to us and complained about how crowded the supermarket was. Felicia quickly tried to wipe her face, but it didn't work. When Sabrina saw her, she instantly looked worried. "What's wrong with you two?"

I guess it didn't take much for her to figure that we were in a deep conversation. Felicia and I remained quiet. She dropped her bags.

"Don't give me the silent treatment," she said, "What's going on?"

Sabrina's eyes darted from Felicia to me and back to Felicia. I was afraid to speak. I didn't know if I should lie or tell the truth.

Then Felicia blurted, "You know, don't you?"

"Know what?" asked Sabrina.

Felicia curled her lips and said nothing. At first, Sabrina looked away, like she was considering whether she should own up to what she knew. Then, she nodded her head.

"Why wouldn't you tell me?" Felicia asked.

"It wasn't my place," Sabrina replied. By this time, I wondered if I should leave, but I thought that if neither of them said anything to me, I would just keep quiet and let them talk.

"How did you find out?" Sabrina asked.

"I have my ways." Sabrina chuckled.

Felicia kept probing until Sabrina reluctantly admitted that the sale was going very well. In fact, Felicia's dad had a buyer. I've never seen Felicia look as afraid as she did then. I was afraid, and not just for Felicia, but for me, too. What would the sale mean for my dad and me? For Felicia, the sale was for something special, at least that's what Sabrina insisted. Felicia didn't want to hear that. I had a hard time understanding that myself. But Sabrina was very convincing as she kept defending Felicia's dad's decision. The hotel was costing too much to keep open.

"What could be more important than this place? My mother worked hard for it, and he knows that. I mean, he was right next to her building it," Felicia cried. Her pain was all over her face. And so was Sabrina's.

She pleaded with Felicia to go to her dad and let him explain everything. "Will you please talk to him tonight?"

Felicia was reluctant, but she finally agreed. I wanted more than anything to hear the conversation with her dad, instead of being around my own. My dad's great mood should have been a good thing. The problem was, I was worried about my friend, but I couldn't tell him I had a friend in Felicia, let alone explain my concern for her. And that wasn't fair. I felt alone again, but for the first time, I felt it even when I was with him. As much as I thought about Felicia, I needed her too. I still desperately wanted to find out about *my* family.

Chapter Six

The next day, I helped Felicia wipe down the lobby as she gave me the details of her talk with her father the night before. I didn't know that much about him, but after she was done, I felt like I had known Felicia's dad for years. He's a nice man who pretty much allows Felicia to do whatever she wants. That's not to say he didn't care about her, it's just he was so different from my dad. I know she's older than me, but Felicia's dad trusts her more than my dad ever trusted me. He even let her run the hotel the way she wanted. But he wasn't going to let Felicia change his mind. Sabrina was right. The hotel had been sold and the money was for Felicia to go to college.

"He said I could go wherever I wanted." She didn't seem too happy about it. I knew how bad she felt, but I also thought she was lucky that her dad not only said she could choose where to go, but he was also giving her the money to do it. All I did was ask my dad if could I go away, and he couldn't even talk about it.

"So, are you going to go?"

Felicia shrugged her shoulders.

"You should," I said. "Didn't you say you would study hotel management?"

"Yeah, but not like this." She kept wiping the windows. I wasn't sure why we were cleaning when it wouldn't be long before everything would be gone, but I continued dusting the table.

"You know, my mom picked out these drapes."

I looked at them. I could tell they were nice at one time, but now they looked as ragged as one of Ms. Baxter's old bathrobes. Felicia sat down and looked around the lobby. She said her father showed her the actual amount of money he spent each month to keep the hotel open versus how much they were getting from people like my dad and me to stay there. It wasn't good. Felicia even proposed to her dad that she work part time at another place besides the hotel, but her dad said it was too late for that. Her dad was smart. He sold the place without her knowing because he knew she would try to come up with some way to keep it open.

"When will it really close?" I asked, a little scared of the answer.

"My father wants everything cleared out in two months." She was quiet for a minute. "I know my father is right." She said it so low, I could hardly hear her. "It's just that this was my mom's place, you know what I mean?"

Even though I didn't have a mother, I did know what she meant. Felicia wiped her eyes and, as she had done before, abruptly changed the subject.

I didn't push her to keep talking about something that made her so upset. She let me vent. I actually appreciated it. She listened and promised me that we would continue the search for my family. Then it was almost time for my dad to return from work. Just as Felicia and I left the cleaning rags in the office, Sabrina walked in with a customer. I thought about her. I wondered if Felicia cared about what Sabrina would do.

Would she find another place to work, or would she just stop all together? As Felicia gave Sabrina the keys to a room, Sabrina put her hands over Felicia's and said she was going to be okay. Then, as she began to walk away with the guy, Sabrina stopped and told him she would be right with him. She turned to us and said to me, "There was something I wanted to tell you yesterday, Jasmine. I saw someone who looked just like you. Well, not really *someone*. It was a picture."

"Me?" I asked.

Felicia asked her where.

"Actually," Sabrina laughed, "It was on a flyer at the market. It was on a bulletin board right near the exit doors. You looked just like this missing girl."

I giggled while she continued.

"There was a picture on one side of the flyer of a three-year-old girl and then on the other side was this computer image of what the girl would look like today, and I swear the image looked just like you. Isn't that creepy?"

I started laughing. "Oh, yeah, that *is* creepy," I said, "But she can't look too much like me because I'm not missing."

Felicia wasn't laughing and she interrupted us, "You'd better go, Sabrina. Jasmine has to get back to her room anyway."

"Oh that's right," Sabrina said, winked her eye, and walked away.

I wanted to see the picture. I thought it would be fun.

"You'll get your chance," Felicia said. I could see her mind working as she started to walk into the office. She turned on the computer, and I asked her what she was doing. She wouldn't answer, so I kept pushing her. While her computer started up, she turned to me.

"Did it ever occur to you, Jasmine, that you *could* be the girl in that picture?"

"What?" I laughed. "No way. My dad is a whole lot of things, but he wouldn't do that. I told you before he's no criminal."

"Don't be so naïve. It would explain a lot."

Felicia made me real mad. I'm not stupid and I told her so.

"I didn't call you stupid, Jasmine, but *think*. Your father is too secretive. I knew girls in school whose parents were overprotective and none of them were as strange as your father."

I didn't care about the other girls. And I didn't appreciate Felicia calling my dad strange, even though I knew he was. Besides, I'm younger than those high-school girls, so naturally my dad would want to keep me safe.

"Safe, yes," she responded when I defended him, "Away from everybody and everything, no."

"He doesn't keep me from everybody and everything."

Now it was Felicia's turn to laugh. "Your father keeps you up in the room unless he's with you. You said you haven't seen that picture of your mother for a year. You asked me to help you find your family because he won't tell you anything. You have to hide to talk to me. And he paid me to look after you. Remember, you just gave me a list of his strange behavior."

"All right," I snapped. "I know what he's done. So, he's keeping something secret from me, but that doesn't mean he kidnapped me."

Felicia rolled her eyes and started working on the computer. I reminded her that this was *my* dad and that I should know him better than she did.

She ignored me while I rambled on and then, still facing the computer, she said, "This could take a few minutes. I'll let you know what I find out. You better get back to the room. Your *fabulous father* who you know so well will be home soon and you could get in trouble for just talking to a friend."

I sharply turned around. I was even madder at Felicia because she was right. I *did* have to sneak. I always had to creep around like I was doing something wrong, when most times I wasn't. And why *couldn't* I have a friend? I had to pick up my pace as I moved through the hotel hallway to get to the room quickly so I wouldn't have to hear my dad yell at me for just talking to Felicia.

She was smart—what if she was right about this? I got into the room and sat in the chair, but couldn't keep still. My head began to hurt, and so did my stomach. The room was quiet, but I didn't want to watch television, a first for me. And I didn't want to think that my dad could possibly do something so wrong as to kidnap me and that, if he had, *why?* I thought at first it might have been for a good reason. He *did* say that his family and my mom's family didn't care. Maybe he took me from them. But that didn't make sense. If they didn't care, why would he need to take me from them? My stomach really started to turn when I thought of Mrs. Warner and Ms. Baxter. My dad had asked Ms. Baxter and Felicia to do the same thing. Did he pay Ms. Baxter, too? Why would he need to? He never liked Rachel's dad, who was definitely nosy, but could it be that my dad didn't like his *questions* rather than not like *him?* And what about us leaving home right after our pictures were in the newspaper, not to mention the many times we'd moved before then? I got a lump in my throat. I jumped up from the chair out of nervousness and I walked around the room. I started talking out loud, asking the questions I was so afraid of. *Dad, did you really do this? Where am I really from? Where is our family? Who did you take me from?*

It was like my dad was in the room with me. I began to get dizzy, so I sat down. I started crying. I covered my face. I was embarrassed. I trusted my dad so much. I knew that he loved me, so there had to be a good reason for everything, right? He was not a bad man, but I was feeling as convinced as Felicia that I was the missing girl whose photo Sabrina had seen. It all fit. I loved my dad and if it was true, I wouldn't want anything to happen to him. And if it was true, what *would* happen to him? Maybe Sabrina had it wrong. Maybe Felicia would see that I looked nothing like that girl. *But what if it is me? What will I do then?*

I was breathing hard. I tried to calm down. Felicia said she would let me know what she found out. But I was already anxious. I wiped my eyes just as my dad came in, smiling, like he always did.

He said, "Hi, sweetheart."

And I said "Hi." I felt like I almost yelled it, because I was too shaken to want to speak at all.

"Are you okay?" he asked me.

I told him I was, but he wasn't convinced. "It's just girl stuff, Dad. Nothing to worry about." I certainly wasn't going to mention anything to him. There was still the chance it wasn't true.

"Hey," he said, "I saw this Chinese restaurant on the way here. Let's go out to eat. Would you like that? Maybe you'll feel better."

By then, he was in the bathroom, washing up and

changing his clothes. I managed to say dinner was fine, and then whispered to myself to relax. I really wanted to call Felicia, but I couldn't do anything but wait.

As my dad and I walked through the lobby to go to the restaurant, I turned to look at Felicia, but she wasn't at the front desk. No one was there, and the office door was cracked open. Was she still online, checking on me? I wished I could run in to see.

At the restaurant, it seemed like everyone was looking at me when my dad and I sat down at our table. I could have sworn an older couple talked about me. *Do they go to the same supermarket as Sabrina? Do they wonder if that girl is me?* The sick feeling in my stomach came over me again, but I ordered and then ate as much food as I could. My dad was in a talkative mood again. In the middle of dinner, he said what I had dreaded. He had found two apartments and he wanted me to look at them.

"I'm letting *you* decide where we live."

I forced a smile with everything I had in me, but it didn't work.

"What's the matter?" he asked. "I would think you'd be glad I'm leaving this grown-up decision to you."

I giggled a little and said, "I am, Dad. When do we go and look at them?"

He said we would go the next day, with the hope that within the next week we would be in our own place.

"That fast?" I asked. As much as I hated our room at the hotel, I hated the thought of leaving Felicia more.

"Of course," Dad said, sounding surprised. "Aren't you ready for your own room?"

Pretend again, I thought to myself. I acted excited. I faked it as much as possible. Somehow, it worked and somehow I got through dinner. I was fidgety the whole ride back, barely listening to my dad describe each apartment. It was like I was moving in slow motion when we went inside the hotel. Felicia was at the desk. It was all over face. She knew something. She nodded her head and used her hands to signal me to call her. I understood—*the photo was me*. I thought I would throw up everything I had just eaten, right there in the middle of the lobby floor. I kept swallowing, trying to keep my food down. I was very, very afraid. When we reached the room, I asked my dad if I could have a soda. I desperately needed to call Felicia and, besides, I wanted something to settle my stomach. He went and I ran to the phone.

"It's you, Jasmine. I saw the picture." Her voice was weird.

"Are you sure?" I felt panicked, like I might pass out.

"I'm positive. It's definitely you," she said. "It took a little time but I found it on a missing children's website."

I grabbed the trash can just in time as everything I ate for dinner came up. My mouth had a nasty, bitter taste of the broccoli, rice, and chicken I'd eaten.

"Hey, Jasmine, you okay?"

"Mmm, hmm," I mumbled. I wiped my mouth with my hand and asked Felicia what the website said about me, but at that moment my dad walked up to the front desk and asked Felicia for change to use in the vending machine. She put down her cell phone and I could hear them talking. I started to bite my nails, and I never bite my nails.

"Your dad is on the way up," Felicia said. She kept talking fast. "You were kidnapped in Philadelphia."

"What? Philadelphia? How?" I asked.

"I don't know how, but the last contact your family had was when you were three."

"I need to see the picture," I said.

"Okay, I'll show you tomorrow as soon as your dad leaves for work. And there's something else about your father, Jasmine..."

I hung up the phone. My dad was coming in.

"Here you go, sweetheart," my dad said as he gave me the can of soda. "What happened?"

He saw the liquid mixture of what I just eaten in the bottom of the trash can. I told him that my stomach was upset. He put the back of his hand over my forehead, saying I wasn't warm. I held my breath so he wouldn't know I was shaking. I looked at my dad, wondering why he did it, why he had kidnapped me. I wanted to ask him, but I was so scared, and I wanted to see the picture myself to make sure. I still didn't want to believe it. I decided that once I saw the image and knew that it was me, I would make my dad tell me the truth. And then I could find out what more Felicia had to tell me. It couldn't have been anything too awful. I had to let myself believe that.

My dad told me to go to bed. I didn't even argue. I fought to act normal. He tucked me under the covers and got on his knees next to my bed. He stroked my hair. It felt so soothing, so warm. I looked at him. He smiled. He talked quietly and told me not worry, that he would always take care of me. He'd done that so many times before. He could be so caring. Felicia might think my dad was the strangest dad she'd ever seen, and she might be right. But he was the only dad I had. I closed my eyes and tried to remember being three years old. I tried to remember day care, and I couldn't. I could only go as far back as kindergarten, but I could only remember pieces, like my kindergarten teacher, the classroom, and a few places where we had lived. With what Felicia told me, I was left with more questions than ever. If I was from Philadelphia, it would make sense why my dad and I moved around so much. He wouldn't want anyone to find us. As I tried to put things together in my head, I kept acting like I was asleep, until I finally was.

Chapter Seven

In the middle of the night, my dad slammed one of our bags on my bed, then he shook me. "Jasmine, wake up. Get up now." I squinted when he turned on the lights. I sat up to see the other bags packed near the door.

"Get up!" he shouted.

So I did.

"What's wrong, Dad? Why are we leaving?"

"Sweetheart, I know you're not feeling well, but please, not now. Just do what I say."

I stood still and he yelled again for me to move. The clock read 2:20. We were doing it again. We were running. I felt weak.

"Dad, tell me why we're going, please?" I was desperate, and I didn't even try to hide it. He moved around the room quickly. I asked him again to tell me what was happening. He urged me to get dressed.

"Are we leaving because you kidnapped me?"

That sure stopped him, with a shirt in one hand and his shaving kit in the other.

"Where did you get that from?"

I shrugged my shoulders. At first, I wondered if I had made a mistake in asking him the question. But it was too late. I had already blurted out the words.

He walked closer to me and met my eyes and asked me again.

This was it. I decided to let it all out. I told him

everything that I had been thinking all day, of course excluding Felicia, Sabrina, and the picture of me at the supermarket. I had enough to say without including them. My dad became more uneasy with each point I made. When I was done, he didn't say anything for a minute. He looked up, took a deep breath, and hugged me.

"Yes," he said softly, his chin over the top of my head. "I took you, but I had to."

I always wanted the truth from my dad, but I didn't expect him to admit to this. I pulled away from him. I was confused and hurt. He kept talking without me asking him to. He explained that my mother's family was planning to take me away from him in court. "Since your mother was gone, they didn't think I could raise you the right way, or *their* way. So I took you and ran." He asked me to forgive him for lying.

"Why didn't you tell me this before?" Now things started to make sense.

My dad said there were many times he wanted to, but he was afraid I wouldn't understand. He said his family wasn't interested in helping, so he had to do what he had to do.

"You have me, Jasmine. I didn't have anyone. I wasn't sure if I would be able to see you once your mother's family had custody of you. I may have protected you too much, but can you see why?"

I told him yes, because I really could. My dad was brave. If he hadn't taken me, I may not have ever had the chance to know him. There *was* a good reason. And whatever Felicia had to add about my dad, I didn't care. It was probably a lie from my mother's family anyway. I wanted to know more, but my dad told me we had to leave immediately because he thought my mother's family knew where we were now and he'd explain later. So I moved around the room with just as much speed as him.

"Leave that," he said about a few things. We shoved items in bags quickly, in no order. By the time we finished, the room was empty, except a plastic bag that we were going to throw in the trash can outside. It was like we had never been at the hotel.

We nearly ran down the hallway. I asked him about his job, the apartment, where we going. He said not to worry about those things, but he had not decided exactly where we'd live next. I had hoped that maybe Felicia was at the front desk, but I knew she wouldn't be there that late. Instead, her dad was. He had an odd look on his face. He probably wondered why we were leaving in the middle of the night, the same way we had arrived at the hotel. We took all our bags to the car and my dad told me to wait there with the bags. I watched him as he rushed inside for a few minutes, then he ran back out, and we drove off.

On television shows, the police would stop people for driving as fast as my dad did. There wasn't much traffic, but he sped past the cars that were on the road. I looked at the signs—I wanted to know where we were heading. We were going south. I checked out names of the towns we were passing. It seemed we had been driving forever when a car blew its horn really loud. I cried out to my dad. He had drifted into the other lane. He had started to fall asleep while driving. He only said, "Sorry," and we rode for a little while longer, and then he pulled over at a gas station. He told me to stay in the car while he talked to a worker at the gas station. He put gas in the car and he drove again, this time like he knew where he was going.

I was not surprised that my dad and I were soon at another hotel. He said to me, "Just take your toothbrush. We're leaving here after we get some rest."

The place was much worse than Felicia's hotel. You entered all the rooms from outside. The lobby was much smaller. It wasn't really a lobby, just a front desk and a raggedy chair next to a chipped table in a corner. There was a small vending machine against the wall. My dad paid for one room. He was so exhausted, he could barely walk straight. The sky was starting to lighten. It was around 5:30 in the morning when we walked into our room.

"Get some rest, Jasmine," my dad said as he plopped on the bed. He went right to sleep.

I needed to call Felicia. I made sure my dad was sleeping hard. I tiptoed to him. I was so glad he fell on his back, which made it easier for me. I slipped my finger and thumb into his jeans pocket, where he had his phone. I slowly inched it up. My dad shifted a little. I stopped and waited. He breathed heavily. I held my breath and inched up the phone a little more, and a little more, until I had it in my hand. I grabbed the hotel key off the table and tiptoed to the door. I watched my dad as I opened it slowly. I slipped out and went to the front of the hotel to call Felicia. The phone rang until her voice message came on. I hung up and called again. Voice message. I called and hung up about five times. I *had* to reach her. I didn't know how long it would be before I could call again. Finally, Felicia answered.

"Whoever this is calling me better know me and have a good reason."

"Felicia, it's me, Jasmine."

"Jasmine? What's wrong?"

"Nothing, it's just that my dad and I left."

"You *what?*"

I told her everything. "So you see, Felicia, he *had* to take me."

"Jasmine, where are you?" She sounded worried. I told her Florence, South Carolina, the last town name I saw when we left the highway. She asked me for the hotel name and even our room number. I told her. She asked me how long we had been driving. I told her over two hours.

"I'm coming to you," she said.

I asked her why. She said she'd explain it when she saw me, but to just get back to the room.

"What are you worried about, Felicia? My dad told me everything. I'm okay. You don't have to come here."

"Okay, Jasmine. I hear you. I won't come. But do you trust me?"

Of course I did.

"Then just go back to the room and call me again as soon as you can." I didn't understand what her problem was, but I listened to her. I ran back. Suddenly the hotel looked too much like a place where a big, crazy man with a ski mask would jump out of nowhere and chase me. I returned to the room as carefully as I had when I'd left. My dad didn't even move. He was still asleep. I put the keys back on the table. I deleted the calls I made to Felicia and I carefully slipped the phone back into his pocket as much as I could. He slept so hard, he would probably think the phone moved while he was sleeping.

I didn't get undressed. I didn't get under the covers. I lay on my back and looked up at the ceiling that was peeling in some places and cracking in others. I was so tired. I didn't think about anything, not even being in such a crappy hotel.

My dad threw water on his face after he woke me up. I didn't even know when I finally fell off to sleep. Since we were dressed and he had his strength again, he told me to brush my teeth, wash my face, and that we would shower and change our clothes at the next stop.

"Dad, where are we going?"

"I don't know yet." He sat next to me on the bed. He rubbed his head. Even though he just woke up, he sounded tired.

"I'm really sorry if I scared you," he said to me. "I promise, Jasmine, I'm going to find us a really nice place to live and stay." It was time for us to go. It was almost eleven o'clock. For the first time, I felt confident that my dad would keep his promise. We went to the front desk to turn in our key. We walked to the car and when we reached it, suddenly they were there from all directions.

Chapter Eight

Police cars surrounded us.

What did Felicia do? I wanted to scream. *How could she call the police?*

One officer yelled, "Kenneth Turner, put up your hands."

My dad looked at me and said, "I'm sorry baby," and held his hands up like the television criminals I had said he wasn't.

In no time, several officers ran to him and grabbed him. He was pushed onto the hood of the car. My dad looked helpless. I ran over, and hollered that they had the wrong man, that my dad's name was Darryl Hinton.

I put my arms around my dad's neck and held tight. An officer pried my hands off my dad, while my dad screamed at the officer, "Don't hurt her!"

A woman in a pants suit came over and tried to quiet me. I kept crying out to my dad. I heard the officer say to another officer, "Why does she keep calling him dad?"

Everything was happening so fast. They put my dad in a police car and he kept shouting to me that everything would be all right. I heard him until they closed the car door. He kept his eyes on me and he never stopped yelling. I just couldn't hear what he was saying. I was hysterical. I kicked and screamed, until the woman said,

"Jasmine, Jasmine, please, please stop. Let us explain what's happening."

My legs went weak and I fell to my knees. I was so drained. I realized there was nothing I could do *but* stop.

I cried hard in the back seat of a car with the suited woman next to me. She said her name was Ms. Rhodes, but I could call her Terri. Strangely, with everything going on, I still thought about my dad telling me to always refer to adults with a title. Ms. Terri, as I called her, said she was an F.B.I. agent. I asked her through my tears where my dad was, and she said she would tell me everything soon. I just cried harder. She moved closer and held me. I didn't even know her, but she rocked me and stroked my hair like she knew me well. I hated to think what her jacket would look like when the car would stop. Tears poured from my eyes and my nose was running. We rode for a while. I kept my eyes closed. *Why did Felicia call the police on my dad?* I never would have thought she would do something like that.

"They have the wrong man," I screamed at Ms. Terri.

"Shhh," she said. "You'll know everything soon."

She didn't agree with me. If she had, she would have said so. Maybe I *was* naïve, like Felicia said. Is this what she wanted to tell me about my dad, that I really wasn't his daughter? The cop had asked why *I* was calling him *Dad*. I wanted it to be like those dreams in television shows. I wanted to wake up and find that everything that just happened wasn't real and I simply had to learn something. But the truth was that I was in a car with an F.B.I. agent who just arrested a man I thought was my dad, but she wouldn't say that he was.

Lisa R. Nelson

I didn't know where we were or where we ended up when the car turned and stopped. When the officer put it in park, Ms. Terri said, "Oh I don't believe this. How did they find out already?"

The officer said, "You have to admit, this is unusual."

What was unusual and why was there so much noise outside? People were talking over each other. I couldn't understand even one word. Ms. Terri began to sit up, so I had to move. As I knew it would be, the one side of her jacket was wet from my tears. She didn't even care. She took it off and said to me softly, "Now Jasmine, I'm going to put this over your head so no one can see you."

Now I could take a good look at her. She was a black woman, around my complexion. Her eyes were a light brown, and she had her hair pinned up. She looked a little older than my dad. I got a quick glance of news reporters with microphones, photo cameras and video cameras all around the car before she put her jacket over my head.

Ms. Terri told the officer who drove and the other one who was in the passenger seat to come to our side and cover us. I couldn't see anything but the black silk lining of her jacket and, as I inhaled, I smelled a sweet perfume that was really nice. My heart was racing. The officer opened the door and then I heard the shouted questions.

"Can you tell us where you found Alexis?"

"Have you made an official arrest?"

"Have you made contact with the family?"

We were walking through what felt like a large crowd, but all I could see from under the jacket were Ms. Terri's legs and my own feet. Ms. Terri had one arm around me tightly, and I could tell she was waving her other one in front of us.

Why are they calling me Alexis? Is that my real name? Who is Kenneth Turner?

The officers opened the doors to a building and Ms. Terri lifted her jacket off me. We were at a police station, and officers were moving around, but they stopped to look at me. It was weird and made me anxious. I tried not to look at anyone, but hoped to see my dad. So much had happened in the last day, I didn't know how to feel. But my stomach turned again. My head felt like it was about to explode, right along with my heart, and I was really tired.

Ms. Terri took my hand as we walked through the station, which was busy with cops. Some men and women didn't have on uniforms, but were wearing suits, and all of them looked at me. I didn't see my dad anywhere. Ms. Terri opened a door to a room that had a square wooden table in the middle and a few wooden chairs around it. She asked me if I wanted anything. I didn't want anything to eat, but I sure was thirsty. She went to get juice. I was left alone, so I went to the corner of the one window in the room and peeked through the closed blinds. The reporters were still outside. Some were sitting on steps, others were on cell phones. I watched them, but made sure they couldn't see me.

"They're still hanging out there, huh?"

I jumped.

Ms. Terri apologized for frightening me. It was okay. There wasn't too much she could do to rattle my nerves any more than they had been. Just then another woman came into the room. This woman had on a shirt with a pair of pants. She was white with dark hair. She looked close to Mrs. Warner's age. Ms. Terri told me her name was Ms. Carter, but I could call her Ann. Ms. Terri brought me a cranberry juice and a doughnut that an officer got for me from a truck outside. She wanted me to try and eat. I didn't want to. I wanted to know where my dad was.

Ms. Terri and Ms. Ann sat next to me and assured me that all my questions would be answered. Ms. Ann was a social worker, and she said she wanted me to express myself any way I felt the need to, because I would learn some things that might be hard to hear. For a little while the two of them went back and forth to prepare me for some heavy news that neither was saying yet. They kept comforting me before I knew why.

I kept still and quiet. The fear in me was strong—so strong I jumped again when there was a knock on the door. Ms. Terri went out of the room for a few minutes, and then she returned to tell me they were bringing my dad in to talk to me. I ran to him as he came through the doorway. We held each other, and I cried hard in his arms. I began coughing. He cried as well. I could feel his body shake. We didn't separate until a police officer, who I hadn't noticed at first, tapped my dad on his shoulder. My dad took my hand and we sat down next to each other. Ms. Terri and Ms. Ann went to the other chairs. The officer stood by the door. I didn't understand why he was there—my dad wasn't dangerous. He'd never hurt anybody. Ms. Ann asked if my dad wanted to begin. He turned his chair around so we could face each other.

I was even more nervous now. I took a sip from my juice, but my mouth was still dry. This was serious. I would finally know the truth and I wasn't sure if I was ready.

My dad took my hands. They were shaking. So were his. He rubbed them and stared at them before saying anything. The room was quiet. Everyone seemed to be waiting to hear what he would tell me, although I suspected they already knew. My dad cleared his throat, but it didn't matter. His voice still quivered.

"I'm so sorry, Jasmine. I, uh," his voice faded and he cleared his throat again. He still wouldn't look at me. He struggled to speak and then he said, "I lied to you."

He shifted in his chair and tears starting streaming down his face again. His eyes were red, too red for having just started crying. My breathing got very intense. I had never seen him so upset.

"I told you I took you, but I lied about why and how it was done."

My dad's voice cracked when he confessed to me that he was my uncle, my real mother's brother. His name was Kenneth Turner, and mine was Alexis Turner.

"How could you be my uncle?" I asked. "I don't understand."

I felt heat rush to my face. My stomach really started spinning. My dad—rather, my uncle—reluctantly looked at me. He tried, but quickly looked away and shifted again in his seat. I was trying to take in what he told me.

All that time, I had been feeling pity for a man who I *knew* was my dad. To me, he was the dad of a girl, which I thought was harder than being one of a boy. Like, the first day I had my period, he was so uncomfortable. Luckily, we had talked about it in health class and Rachel had hers before me, so I knew what to expect. But who I thought was my dad still managed to talk to me about it, even if he was clumsy and nervous about it. He even lectured me for days that I couldn't date for a long time because he was afraid that I would get pregnant. And I remembered how he tried, sometimes muttering curse words, to untangle my hair before he realized he had no business trying to wash and style it himself. But we both got through it.

Now, after those things and so many others, he told me that he wasn't my dad after all. *Could he have kidnapped me to save me from something? Why else would he take me?* He'd always been like a dad to me. He took care of me, no matter what. He could have left me to fend for myself. But he didn't. He didn't touch me in the wrong places. He didn't abuse me. He didn't leave me without food or clothes. And he wasn't strange at all. He was just trying to keep this secret in order to protect me. There had to be a good reason for what he did. Something must have been wrong with my mom's family to make him take me.

I started asking him questions like, "You were protecting me from my mom's family, right? You had to do it, didn't you? You were keeping me from trouble, weren't you?"

He shook his head harder with each question. "No, Jasmine," he interrupted. "That's not it at all."

I never really got used to being without a mother. I thought I had, until I talked with Felicia about hers. I was alone a lot before coming to Raleigh. When I watched family shows, I imagined I was one of the kids being held like Ms. Terri held me in the car. I hated coming home from school and needing to talk to someone or being excited about passing a test, but my dad was always at work. Sharing my day with Ms. Baxter definitely wasn't an option. Even if my dad was home, he wouldn't have wanted to hear about a cute boy I liked, my first kiss, or an outfit I wanted. My mom would have. It was those times when I really missed having one. Somehow, I thought I was okay with it all, but Felicia made me realize that it wasn't okay. And now, in a room with three strangers, my *uncle* tells me that I've had a mother all along, and he kept that from me too.

"My mom's alive?" I struggled to ask.

My uncle nodded silently.

"Jasmine, you have to know I never wanted to hurt you. I love you too much."

My mind drifted. My dad's—my *uncle's* voice became muffled. I didn't hear his pleas for my forgiveness. I only saw the desperation in his face. All my life he had me to himself. He fooled me, even the night before in Felicia's hotel. Each Thanksgiving we cooked and ate together. Every Christmas, he had gifts for me and we spent the day at home. I made him gifts at school for Father's Day and he always bought me something I wanted for my birthday. No matter what we did, it was always just the two of us, and he loved it that way. But now I knew that he had taken my mom away from me. *How could I have been so stupid?* Felicia always knew something bizarre was going on, and I didn't want to believe her. I suspected something strange before I met her and should have done something about it. I stared at the doughnut. I couldn't move or scream or shout, although I wanted to.

"Jasmine, Jasmine," Ms. Ann's voice jolted me. *Why is she calling me Jasmine? Isn't my name Alexis? Should I just start using it like Jasmine never existed? Isn't my life like some fantasy for my uncle? Jasmine, a name he created, a life he built, always controlling my every move?*

"Where is she? Where's my mom?" I asked sharply. This man, whoever he was to me now, looked at Ms. Terri and Ms. Ann, as if they knew and he didn't.

"We should stop," Ms. Ann recommended. I pleaded that we keep going. I told them that if there was more for me to know, I could handle it. Did they think they knew me? They didn't know Jasmine Hinton. They had no way of knowing what I could or couldn't handle. So they agreed that I hear it all. I looked back at my dad. Uncle Kenneth. It was obvious that he was afraid to continue. All the pieces came together at once. He finally couldn't get out of revealing the whole truth.

There were three of them. My uncle Kenneth, the oldest, my aunt Celeste, who is five years younger, and my mom, Robin, two years younger than Aunt Celeste. They all grew up in Philadelphia with their parents, my grandparents. They made a pact, Uncle Kenneth, my mom, my real dad, and my Aunt Celeste, when I was born. My mom had me when she was a teenager, so I was supposed to be raised by relatives, but my parents didn't want that. The four of them—my real parents, my aunt, and my uncle—spent hours on a plan. My mom cried hard when she kissed me goodbye and gave me to my uncle. My real dad had tears in his eyes, too. There were two cars, Uncle Kenneth's, with me in it, and the other had my mom, my real dad, and my aunt. At a location away from their home, Uncle Kenneth and I drove away with my parents and aunt looking on. Uncle Kenneth was to raise me for a few years until my mom was older and my parents were able to care for me. He then was supposed to return me to them, but he didn't. He raised me for fourteen years. I thought I was from Florida. I thought my birthday was in March. It's actually in October—I'd be fifteen sooner than I originally thought. Almost nothing about my own life was true. At least not what I knew.

I covered my face and cried. I never knew what tears of anger felt like until then. Uncle Kenneth moved closer and put his arms around me. I was too angry to hug him back, but I didn't brush him off, either. It was strange. I was fuming inside. *How could he do this to me?* And then I was also afraid of what would happen next. I'd only had him and I missed him already.

That's when Ms. Ann really stopped everything. Uncle Kenneth fought to stay in the room, but he was eventually escorted out by the officer, still apologizing, telling me he loved me, and begging me to forgive him. I was left in a room with two strangers who knew more about who I was than I did. Even the reporters outside knew who I was. Ms. Terri and Ms. Ann brought in tissues, because I was as hysterical as I had been in the car earlier. I could feel my eyes swelling. They managed to calm me.

"Is my... uncle going to jail?" I was mad, but I didn't think he deserved that.

"We're not sure." Ms. Terri responded softly. "He has to return to Philadelphia and face charges for kidnapping you."

"Is that where I'm going?" The answer was probably yes, but not right away. Ms. Terri and other authorities, those in Philadelphia, were working on contacting my mom. That meant I could actually meet her soon. But would she want to meet me? After all, she gave me to my uncle. What if she had forgotten about me? What if they all had, my real dad, my aunt, and my grandparents? I was a baby when they last saw me. How did Ms. Terri know that any of them would have even wanted to have anything to do with me? What was I supposed to do now?

I felt very alone. I didn't feel like I belonged anywhere or to anyone. Ms. Ann tried to console me. I knew that was her job, but for some reason she seemed sincere. It worked a little. But what really made me smile in the midst of so much agony was when there was another knock on the door, by a man in a suit. Ms. Ann and Ms. Terri, with him, whispered together in the doorway until they all agreed on something. Ms. Terri then came over to me to tell me that Felicia was there to see me and that they would allow her to visit, but we didn't have long.

I was so relieved. The door opened and Felicia, Sabrina, and Felicia's dad came in together. Felicia ran to me and hugged me tightly. I cried again. She apologized for calling the police, but she didn't have to. How would I have found out about everything if she hadn't? And who knows where we would be now? For the first time, I really felt how much Felicia cared about me. And not only her—Sabrina and Felicia's dad stood next to me, asking if I was okay and if I needed anything. Suddenly, I didn't feel so deserted.

We sat down, since Ms. Terri and Ms. Ann gave us a few minutes to talk.

Sabrina whispered to me, "You know this is not exactly where I'd like to be right now, but for you, I'm making the sacrifice." She smiled at me.

I giggled for the first time in what seemed like forever. I told them about my uncle, who they already knew about. And I told them my real name.

"Alexis is a cool name," Felicia said and winked. I smiled again. I asked Felicia if the news about my uncle was what she wanted to tell me. It was. She decided to keep it from me when I called her after my dad—my uncle—and I left.

"I just knew you would have panicked," she said.

She was right—I would have.

"Who would've ever thought something like this would happen?" Felicia's dad asked.

"I had a feeling something was strange by the way he acted," Sabrina added.

It seems that when my uncle woke me up in the middle of the night, he had just come from another trip to the vending machine for a soda for himself. He saw Sabrina and she told him about my picture at the supermarket. She thought it was something funny to share with him. That's when everything spiraled out of control. My uncle didn't even finish his conversation with her. She said he looked shocked and quickly walked away.

"Have you seen him?" Felicia asked.

I nodded. "My mom's alive," I blurted.

"She's alive?" Felicia asked.

"Oh, wow," Sabrina said. Felicia's dad was also surprised. But Felicia's mood changed.

"The description about your kidnapping just said your uncle took you away from your family. It didn't say anything about you having a mother," Felicia added.

Her dad and Sabrina kept telling me about it. Felicia remained quiet and even looked away.

"I won't know how to act if I see her," I said.

"If?" Felicia's dad asked.

I explained I wasn't sure if she'd want to see me. He and Sabrina told me not to worry about any of that. Felicia didn't say anything.

"What should I do, Felicia?" I needed to hear from her.

"Don't worry. It'll all come naturally." She said it so quickly, it sounded rehearsed. I wanted her to say more to me. I needed her to give me advice like she always had.

"That's it? Should I say something special to her?"

Felicia told me to just be myself and that I would know what to say. Then she was silent again.

"Is anything wrong, Felicia?"

"No. Why?" She didn't look at me.

"You usually have more to tell me than that."

"There's nothing more to say." She was curt and that was it. I looked at Sabrina as if to ask if she knew what happened. She gave me a "don't worry" expression. She and Felicia's dad changed the subject.

"You've become a real celebrity. There are reporters all over the place," Felicia's dad joked.

Ms. Ann and Ms. Terri looked up. They had been in a corner of the room, seemingly not paying us any attention. But they had all along. They eased closer to us.

"Yeah," Sabrina added, "You're all over the news."

"I am?"

And that's when Ms. Terri and Ms. Ann cut in. It was time for me to go. Where, I didn't know. I wanted more time, but I had the upsetting feeling that Felicia had had enough. Before they left, we all exchanged hugs, although Felicia's was noticeably gentler than the one she gave me when they came in. She struggled to say that she would wait to hear from me. In fact, her voice wavered a little.

Sabrina whispered that she knew what was wrong and that she would talk to Felicia. "It'll be okay," she told me.

I was sad when the door closed behind them. I would have rather stayed with them, but they weren't family, even though I knew all of them better than my real family.

Protected by Ms. Terri, Ms. Ann, and police officers, I rode hidden in a car past the reporters, without them noticing, to the house where I would stay for the next four days. The house was under the Department of Social Services, a home where children like me stayed, those who were displaced. Ms. Terri and Ms. Ann explained to me that the owners of the home were a married couple who had taken care of children for more years than I'd been alive. Their names were Mr. and Mrs. Sutler. We drove up to the large house, which was surrounded by a wide front yard and two big trees. They came to the door together. They were older, like grandparents, and the color of a chocolate milkshake. They were immediately friendly toward me, but I wasn't in the mood to meet them. I wasn't interested in staying at yet another place, especially alone, and I was afraid. As nice as they were, I thought to myself, were Ms. Ann and Ms. Terri actually going to leave me with these people—a couple of strangers?

The house had four bedrooms, plus Mr. and Mrs. Sutler's room, which was always closed off. There was a large backyard, a living room with a mantle full of pictures, a dining room, and a kitchen. I'd never been in house so huge. There was only one other child in the house, Melanie, and she was about six months old. She looked like she could be Felicia's child.

When Ms. Ann and Ms. Terri left, Ms. Ann promised to see me every day.

And she did. The next day she took me to a doctor, who gave me a full examination. I had never had that before. Uncle Kenneth only took me to the doctor twice, once when I had a bad cough from a cold and another time when my hearing was muffled from an infection.

Ms. Ann told me that my visit to the doctor's office had gone fine. I went to the eye doctor and the dentist as well. My eyes were perfect, but I had two cavities, which Ms. Ann said would be handled later.

Ms. Terri came over one of the days I was at the Sutler's to question me about my uncle.

I felt like I was snitching on him. It was the way Ms. Terri phrased her questions. But everything I told her was true. I did spend lots of time by myself. And we did move around often, staying at all kinds of cheap hotels. And neither my uncle nor I had many friends. Hardly any. I tried to convince Ms. Terri that it wasn't that bad for me, even though I had to admit, if only to myself, that it often was. I even asked if she spoke with Ms. Ann about my doctor's appointments. If my uncle was really so terrible, wouldn't they have found more things wrong with me than just two cavities? I wasn't sure that Ms. Terri was convinced. She ignored my question and I couldn't read what she thought from the expression on her face. She seemed emotionless as she jotted notes of everything I said. I only hoped that I didn't make my uncle's case worse.

Chapter Nine

I stayed at the Sutlers' while Ms. Ann, Ms. Terri, and other authorities located my family. My uncle's car was still at the police station. I wasn't sure when I would get used to calling him that. Ms. Ann was able to get some clothes for me out of the car. Mr. and Mrs. Sutler turned out to be the kind of grandparents I would probably want. Mrs. Sutler spent a lot of time caring for Melanie, who spent a lot of her time laughing. I helped Mrs. Sutler, who did just about all of the talking. She never asked me about my life, and I appreciated that. She let me talk when I wanted, which only was to ask basic things like where was the bathroom and could I have more to drink. She didn't make me say anything more than that.

Mr. Sutler let me help him with his garden. I liked that. It gave me a chance to watch birds. He didn't make me talk either. Instead, he told me about how he liked to play outside when he was a little boy, and he taught me about his garden like I was his personal student. We pulled weeds and he gave me the hose to water the lawn. We didn't stay outside in the middle of the day because it was early August and very hot outside. Thank goodness they had cool air-conditioning in the house.

Mrs. Sutler could really cook, and we ate at the kitchen table at the same time for each meal. I would listen to Mr. and Mrs. Sutler talk about the news, their neighbors, and their family. On the mantle were pictures of their four children and nine grandchildren. Melanie would chime in at dinner with her goo-goo, gaa-gaa stuff. I liked Melanie. I would feed her, change her, and play with her when Mrs. Sutler was doing laundry or cleaning up. My days were spent that way. Mr. and Mrs. Sutler let me sleep as long as I wanted, but I was usually awakened by the smell of bacon or sausage every morning. They would be at the table with Melanie in a high chair by the time I came down to the kitchen. There was always plenty to eat. Even during the day, Mrs. Sutler had fruit in a bowl on the dining room table and she sometimes let me have a few cookies between meals. On the third day I was there, I offered to help Mrs. Sutler set the table for dinner. That was her chance to tell me about how she grew up with eight brothers and sisters. I couldn't imagine that many people living in one house at the same time.

"And our house wasn't even this big," she said, as she put food on our plates. It was always interesting listening to the Sutlers' stories. It took my mind off my own story. They made me laugh, like the time Mr. Sutler was chased by a neighbor's dog.

"My mother told me to stay away from him. But I didn't listen. I kept throwing sticks and rocks over his fence. Then one day, I didn't know the latch was off the gate. That little dog had had enough of me and he chased me until I had to climb a tree. He ripped the bottom of my pants and circled that tree, while I screamed for help, knowing there was nobody around. I wouldn't come down either, even after I wet my pants. Everyone was looking for us and it wasn't until night-time when they found us. I never bothered that dog again. In fact, I never went anywhere near that house."

Mrs. Sutler said she laughed every time she heard the

story. We all laughed, even Melanie, like she understood. Funny thing was, I stayed with the Sutlers during the day instead of keeping to myself. They kept me busy and I enjoyed it, because I didn't want to think. I didn't want to remember my own stories right now. The only time I thought about me was at night, in bed. The house was very quiet during those hours. I would look around the room at the dressers, which were old but in good condition, the paintings of children and meadows on the walls, and then I would turn to my side and stare out the window at the dark night.

Rummaging through my bag of clothes each day, I could tell either Ms. Ann or Ms. Terri had removed my uncle's things. But they couldn't have known that one of my shirts was a gift he gave me for my first day of school. I cried myself to sleep that night, thinking about him, and again the second night, when I found Mrs. Warner's phone number still buried where I had hidden it deep in my small purse. I tried not to, but I still wanted my uncle to be my dad. I had told Felicia it was okay that she had called the police. But would it have been better if I had stopped asking him questions and just accepted things as they were? We would still be together and I would just think that my dad was a little strange. But then, I had to remember that there might be a whole family that I knew nothing about and that my uncle had kept them from me.

I cried again, worried about what Ms. Ann and Ms. Terri would find out about my family. Was my mom's family nice? What about Aunt Celeste? Would I have to move to Philadelphia? Who would I live with? I guess it would have to be my mom. Philadelphia wasn't so far away, I told myself. I wouldn't mind living with Felicia, if I could. But then again, after the way she acted when I last saw her, I wasn't sure we were still friends. Besides, she may have decided to go to college. When I thought about it, I had no one.

I couldn't find out anything about myself. Mr. and Mrs. Sutler had done a great job in keeping any newspapers out of the house. There wasn't a television downstairs or in any of the bedrooms. I had no way of knowing what was going on in the world. I asked if I could call Felicia, but Mrs. Sutler told me kindly that I couldn't call anyone yet.

One afternoon, Mrs. Sutler yelled for me to bring the pack of diapers that were in a shopping bag in the kitchen to her upstairs. Mr. Sutler had dropped off groceries before going out to run more errands. Melanie had made a mess in her diaper and Mrs. Sutler had to give her a quick bath. I did what Mrs. Sutler asked, and as I stood in the bathroom doorway, I looked up the hall and saw that Mr. and Mrs. Sutler's bedroom door was slightly open. I slowly moved away while Mrs. Sutler took care of Melanie and quietly made my way to their room. I couldn't have cared less about their room, although it was large and beautiful, with a dresser and mirror against one wall, a huge four-poster bed, four long windows, and a rug on the floor under the bed. I just wanted to see if they had a television—and they did. I grabbed the remote that was next to the bed and turned it on. I went close the screen, immediately pressed the low-volume button just enough so I could hear it, and clicked the channel button until I found the news network. After two segments and one commercial, I saw a picture that must have been what Sabrina and Felicia saw. It was me! I finally saw it for myself. I saw myself at three years old. I didn't remember the clothes or where I was, but I was still just a baby. Right after that, they showed a picture of my uncle. He looked worse than I had ever seen him. But it was after he was arrested, and a mug shot is not exactly the kind of picture someone would pose for. They even showed when I was escorted by Ms. Terri into the police station. The reporter mentioned that I was fourteen and from Philadelphia, that Uncle Kenneth kidnapped me and was still in custody, and that the authorities were waiting for the DNA test to come back from my parents.

"Oh my God, Jasmine! You shouldn't be watching that, honey!" Mrs. Sutler ran to me with Melanie in her arms and grabbed the remote. She shut off the TV. I didn't say anything. I was in shock. They had found my parents. I forgot I was in Mrs. Sutler's room and I sat down on her bed. She was muttering about how things were messed up now, how this was the first time anything like this happened, and how she was always so careful. I barely heard her. She quickly pulled me up and we went downstairs. While Melanie played with toys in her playpen, Mrs. Sutler was on the phone with Ms. Ann, frantically telling her what had just happened. I wasn't mad at Mrs. Sutler, and I hoped Ms. Ann wouldn't be either. I was strangely excited and terribly afraid at the same time. Why would Ms. Ann and Ms. Terri keep this from me? I jumped up and went to Mrs. Sutler when she hung up the phone.

"What did she say?" I asked.

Mrs. Sutler rubbed her hands together. She was still upset. "Ann's coming over right now. I'm going to let her talk to you." Then she offered me some cookies, juice, fruit, even leftovers from dinner the night before. I realized it was all she could offer to mend something I didn't think needed mending. I didn't want anything. She looked at me worriedly as I plopped down on the couch near Melanie. I watched her play while I waited. I was a baby just like her once. Uncle Kenneth had said I was a happy one. I didn't know how Melanie ended up at the Sutlers, but I hoped that, for her sake, she would find out who she was long before I had.

I was restless on that couch. Mrs. Sutler sat with me, but I was quiet until the doorbell rang. Ms. Terri was with Ms. Ann. Mrs. Sutler apologized over and over, but they reassured her and asked to be alone with me. She took Melanie and left us in the living room.

I didn't hold back. I came right out and asked if they had found my parents.

They had. They didn't want to scare me in case they weren't found. But the DNA test, they explained to me, the blood test to determine who my parents are, had come back. They told me that my mother was on a plane, on her way to meet me, and that my father would see me in Philadelphia.

"Is there anything you want to say?" Ms. Ann asked me. I was silent for a while.

"Did you talk to her? Did you talk to my mom?" I asked.

Ms. Terri said she had. I asked her how my mother sounded.

"She sounds very nice. She never married, and you're her only child."

Did that mean she really wanted to meet me? She had to if she was flying here. Or did she feel that she was obligated because I was all over the news?

How did my father feel? My *real* dad? I started to get shaky all over. It's not that I was afraid to go to a new place. I had gotten used to moving from place to place. I was more scared about meeting my parents. After all, they were total strangers. Suddenly, I missed my dad— my uncle—more than ever.

Ms. Terri had said my mom sounded nice. Did that mean she was? How many people were in my family? Ms. Terri and Ms. Ann decided to let my mom answer these questions. I just couldn't believe it was all happening. *My mom was on her way.* I would meet her the next morning. I had so much to ask her about, if she was interested. I thought I would know immediately if she wasn't. This wasn't like the first day of school and wondering about the new teacher and if I would have a good school year. And it wasn't built up like when I shook a gift box and tried to guess what it was. This was much bigger, much more frightening, and even more surprising. I wish I had the picture that was in Uncle Kenneth's safe. I wanted to stare at it all night, although I did have it memorized in my mind, like Felicia said I would. But then, a photograph doesn't tell you who a person is. *What was my mother like? What if we didn't get along? What if my dad and I didn't either?* I wasn't sure if we would get along, since every time I thought of my dad, I thought of my uncle.

"What do you think about meeting your mother tomorrow?" Ms. Terri asked me.

"I don't know." It was true.

"It must feel strange to you, because you thought she was dead, but I'll tell you this. When I told her we found you, she cried because she was so happy."

"She was?"

Ms. Terri nodded.

So that must have meant she couldn't wait to see me. Didn't it? I felt a thrill at the possibility. I had only hoped that I wouldn't disappoint her when she met me.

By the time we had dinner that night, Mrs. Sutler felt better. Ms. Terri and Ms. Ann must have told her that she was in the clear. She and Mr. Sutler spent the entire meal trying to convince me how happy I should be that my parents had been found. They didn't have to try so hard. I was excited and nervous. But it was too soon to know if I was happy. Time seemed to have slowed down. It was like Christmas Eve when I was younger. I tossed and turned at bedtime. I don't think I slept more than a few hours. I was up in the morning before everyone, even Melanie. I fished around until I found clothes that matched. I had wished my hair was styled better, but I did the best I could after nights of sleeping on it and no curling iron. Then I packed up everything. I was going to be leaving again, but this time, I was really going home.

I wondered what it would look like. Was it big, like the Sutler's house? Or was it an apartment, like the places I lived in with Uncle Kenneth? Would I have my own bedroom? I should, since my mother didn't have any other children. Where did my real dad live? On TV shows with divorced parents, the mom and dad had bedrooms for the children. Would that be the case for me? I tried to stop myself from thinking so much. I would know everything soon enough.

I was fidgety, so I got dressed and waited in the living room. I walked around, listening to the birds chirping outside. I went to the mantle. There were so many pictures lined across it and hanging on the wall above it. Mrs. Sutler told me that she kept pictures of their children and the children who had stayed at their house over the years. I thought I would ask her if she and Mr. Sutler had a camera. I wanted them to take one of me and include me with all the other children. I had only known them a short time, but I already felt close to them. As I heard them moving around upstairs, I felt sad. I'd miss them. They were so kind to me, and they made my stay at their house easier. I probably would never speak to them again, let alone see them again. Mrs. Sutler told me that sometimes people are in your life for a purpose and, when the purpose is complete, you move on. Staring at all the photographs, I understood what she meant. We were alike in a way. I could have easily had a wall of people I'd met and would never see again. Soon I would be up there, too, and I knew that I would never forget them. Somehow I knew they wouldn't forget me, either.

"Did you really think we would let you leave without taking a picture of you?" Mrs. Sutler asked.

I was so glad. So after breakfast, Mr. Sutler snapped the photo. And right after that, the doorbell rang. It was time.

Chapter Ten

Mr. and Mrs. Sutler seemed as excited as I was. Ms. Terri walked in first, then Ms. Ann, who stretched out her arm as if she was introducing a celebrity. My heart began racing so fast, I thought they would see it beating through my shirt. Then my mother walked in. I frowned at first. She wasn't the woman in the picture. My mom looked worried. I think my expression scared her.

"What's wrong, Jasmine?" Ms. Ann asked me nervously.

"Nothing," I said, sorry that I frowned in the first place. Actually, this woman was much prettier than the one in the picture. "It's just that my uncle showed me a photo of my mom and she looks nothing like her."

Ms. Terri put her arm around me and swore that the woman standing in front of me was indeed my mother. The picture Uncle Kenneth had shown me wasn't real, but another lie. It's no wonder he let me look at the picture only on rare occasions. I felt stupid—again. I hadn't looked to see if I resembled the woman in the picture. Maybe if I had, I would have figured out a long time ago that she wasn't my mother. But this woman not only had the same features as me, but she also looked a lot like Uncle Kenneth. I quickly tried to change my expression. I didn't want to upset her.

When I smiled, she smiled. Her cheeks were higher

than mine, but we had the same round eyes. We were both tall, but she was a little muscular. And she was shapely, which gave me hope for my own skinny body. Her hair was dark and cut short at her neck, like mine, but more stylish. She had on a printed summer skirt, with a pink blouse that matched the skirt. She wore nice sandals and hoop earrings. I really liked her outfit. I hoped she enjoyed shopping. I suddenly imagined us shopping together.

"Hi, Jasmine," she said. She seemed nervous, but I couldn't imagine her being as anxious as I was. It was strange how my name is Alexis, but she called me Jasmine. I wondered if Ms. Terri and Ms. Ann suggested she call me that. When she spoke, I noticed her teeth were perfectly straight. Did she wear braces when she was young? My thoughts kept shifting from one thing to another.

After my mom spoke, everyone looked at me, even Mr. and Mrs. Sutler. Then I noticed that there was another black woman at the door, who was just as tall—I could plainly see she was also a relative. She had to be my Aunt Celeste. There were definite similarities between my mom, my uncle, and the woman in the doorway. I felt like I was on stage and had forgotten my lines. Everyone was quiet and waited for my response. All I could think to say was, "Hi."

Then they all looked at my mother, except the other woman who had come with her. She was still staring at me. My mom asked me how I was and I told her, "Fine." I realized I must have sounded silly with short answers, but these were the only ones that came to my mind.

Ms. Ann relieved my tension by finally closing the door and saying, "Why don't we all sit down?"

My mom and I sat on the couch. My mom's eyes were already beginning to tear up. She looked at me all over, but I didn't feel uncomfortable with it. I found myself doing the same thing to her. I wanted to tell her that I usually had on a nicer top, but the one I was wearing was the only decent one I could find in my bags. And I definitely could have done a better job with my hair. Ms. Terri and the woman I didn't know sat in chairs across from the couch. Mr. and Mrs. Sutler brought in a chair for Ms. Ann, who asked my mom if she was ready, just like she had with Uncle Kenneth.

"Jasmine," she said. "I want you to know I never stopped looking for you."

"*You* were looking for *me*?"

She laughed a little and said yes.

The woman said, "We all were."

I turned to the woman and my mom introduced her as Aunt Celeste.

"She's my sister."

I said "Hi" to her, too, and turned back to my mom, who told me she thought about me all the time.

"I would have thought about you, but my dad, I mean, Uncle Kenneth, said you were dead." Maybe I shouldn't have said that. I began to sweat.

My mom clenched her jaw and Aunt Celeste said, "Yes, we know all about what your Uncle Kenny told you."

Is that what they called him, Kenny? My mom didn't look very happy about it at all, but she said that it didn't matter what he told me. *She* wanted me to know everything about her. She want to know all about me.

"Would you like that?"

I said yes, calmly. My mom seemed nice enough, although I had just met her. It could be that she really was happy to reconnect with me. I had hoped that the whole family would feel the same.

"Oh, I want to show you something," she said and reached in her bag and pulled out a large envelope full of newspaper articles and photographs. The articles were about my uncle taking me. They really had been looking for me. The first pictures were of me as a baby, asleep in my mom's arms, with Aunt Celeste and a young man. When Uncle Kenneth first told me about my mom, I didn't bother to ask how old she was when she had me—or how *young* she was. I was too upset to learn that she even existed.

"Everybody looks so young, and you, too." I didn't mean to say that aloud, but that's when I found out that my mom had me when she was fourteen years old.

"I was exactly your age," she said.

My mouth dropped open.

"You were fourteen?" She let out a big sigh and nodded. I was shocked. I couldn't imagine having a baby now. I hadn't even had a boyfriend yet. But then, how could I? I was never alone long enough with a boy for it to happen. I wondered how my mom and dad managed to do it. And why. She was so young.

My mom was silent. She glanced at Aunt Celeste. They both seemed uncomfortable.

"We snuck around to see each other," my mom said, and she added, "He was older and I was under-age." My dad, Kyle Ross, was a freshman in college when I had been born. My mom showed me a current photo of him on her cell phone. She described him as friendly and gentle, and said he couldn't wait to see me.

In fact, his brother, his brother's one son, and my paternal grandparents were also eager to meet me.

I thought my real dad had a nice smile. He was bald

and had a beard. He was handsome. I wanted to know how he and my mom had met, especially since he was older.

My mom looked at Aunt Celeste again, who answered for her. They had met at a summer office party that included families. Both their fathers worked at the same company.

My mom looked relieved that Aunt Celeste had told the story, but I didn't know why. It sounded simple enough. When my mom found out she was pregnant with me, she decided to tell my grandparents later, so they wouldn't talk her out of having me.

"I wasn't sure how they would respond, so I didn't tell your grandparents anything for a while." She had worn oversized tops and lied to my grandmother for months.

I wondered what my grandparents were like. How did they feel when they found out my mom was pregnant? What did my dad's parents think? My mom didn't say at first. She wanted me to know that they were concerned about me now. She shifted the conversation back to my dad and assured me that he really loved me.

I just nodded. I could only think about Uncle Kenneth. When I take away all the lies and the secrets, my uncle didn't do such a bad job. Did my real dad have what it took to be just as good or better? Why hadn't he married my mom when I was born? I didn't want to let on what I was thinking, but I supposed everyone noticed my expression. I put the cell phone down. I didn't say anything about my real dad. I didn't ask any further questions about him. I had a feeling that everyone was waiting for a reaction, but I didn't have one about him. Instead, I focused again on my mom.

"Were your parents mad when you finally told them?"

My mom paused for second and looked at Aunt Celeste, who shrugged her shoulders. I guess they were wondering why I didn't respond to my real dad's picture. My mom didn't push. She just answered my question. My grandparents were furious, and just like Uncle Kenneth told me, they quickly made plans for me to be raised by relatives who lived in a nearby county.

My mom didn't have to give me details about the pact. Ms. Ann mentioned to everyone that Uncle Kenneth had told me about it. My grandparents called the police to report that my uncle kidnapped me. My mom, my real dad, and my aunt acted as if it was true. Meanwhile, my mom and dad secretly opened a post office box. For three years, Uncle Kenneth sent pictures of me with letters about my first words, my first teeth, the first time I walked, the first time I went to day care. The pictures were in the envelope—Uncle Kenneth had made double prints. I had seen all the pictures before, which is why I had never doubted that Uncle Kenneth was my dad.

"Then the letters stopped coming, and we had no way of reaching him." My mom looked sad as she continued. She visited the post office box every day, wanting something to be there from her brother. The box stayed empty. Then, she said, she began looking for me on her own.

"I was only seventeen, about to graduate from high school, and I was looking for you, instead of thinking about graduation," she said softly.

My mom and my aunt had to reveal to my grandparents what actually happened to me. They were furious all over again. When my dad had finished college and found a job, he paid someone to look for me. Even his parents got involved.

But as the years passed, everyone started to slow

down, except my mom. She even chose to stay in Philadelphia after she went to college, just in case Uncle Kenneth came back with me. She wouldn't stop until Aunt Celeste convinced her that it was time to let go—not quit, but to just let go.

"I felt that if I stopped looking for you, I would be giving up I would be admitting that I'd never see you again."

So she kept the post office box. She may not have visited it every day, but she went a few times a week. "I still have the box," she said, with tears in her eyes.

Aunt Celeste also had to wipe her eyes. My mom had always hoped that I would return to her and she always thought about me. She kept repeating that.

All my grandparents still live in Philadelphia. So do my mom and Aunt Celeste. My dad lives in New Jersey. Aunt Celeste has a husband, Malcolm, and two children, Nathan, seven, and Keisha, five. My mom filled me in about the family for almost two hours. My head was spinning. Then Ms. Ann began to discuss the plans for me again.

I remember having a schedule at home, before leaving for Raleigh. I knew when to get up for school, what time school started, what time lunch was, and what time I was supposed to be home. I ate dinner with Uncle Kenneth. Afterwards, we'd watch TV or play a game. I'd go to bed and do it all over again the next day. Weekends and when school ended were the only times I didn't have a routine to follow.

I couldn't have known it then, but I liked it that way. Since we had left home, everything had been haywire. Time meant nothing. I didn't even know what day or date it was some times. I felt tossed around with the adults being the only ones who knew what was going on.

And here I was again, listening to more arrangements for another night in a strange bed, at another hotel, because the next flight to Philadelphia wasn't until the following day. I had to be flexible again, except this time was different. I didn't feel as frustrated. I didn't feel fearful about escaping from somewhere. I *was* nervous, but this time, I was also a little excited about where I was going.

When we were about to leave, my mom asked if she could hug me. "Or would that make you uncomfortable? It's okay if it's too soon," she said, nervously.

I really didn't know if it *was* too soon. I just knew that I wanted to hug her as well. She embraced me cautiously, like she was afraid to break me, but when I didn't let go, she held me tighter and longer. She stroked my hair, rocked me back and forth, kissed my cheek, then my other cheek, and then my forehead. When we separated, she needed a tissue, which Aunt Celeste had in her hand to give her. My aunt was using one already.

I wasn't crying, but it felt warm to be in my mom's arms.

I hugged Mrs. Sutler, who wiped her eyes, too. I held back tears as I waved to Mr. and Mrs. Sutler from the back of the car Ms. Terri drove. The Sutlers had given me their phone number. I swore to myself that I would keep it and call them.

Ms. Terri was taking me, my mom, and Aunt Celeste to a hotel. Ms. Ann followed us. It was supposed to be a place where the reporters wouldn't find us. I didn't realize that they were still talking about me. How could I? After I had snuck to catch that glimpse of the news, Mr. and Mrs. Sutler had kept their bedroom locked for my last night at their house. I had to admit, Ms. Terri and Ms. Ann had found a great hideout for me. When we pulled up to the hotel garage, I was impressed. After all the cheesy places where Uncle Kenneth and I had stayed, this was something out of a magazine. We went in through the back, to be safe, and we had to wait to make sure everything was clear before we went in. I saw the nice suitcases my mom and Aunt Celeste were carrying, and I was embarrassed by my stuffed duffle bag. My uncle and I never had a set of luggage. We never went on any overnight vacations. Our trips consisted of quickly packing, leaving our home, and staying at a rundown hotel until Uncle Kenneth found us a place to live.

My mom looked at me and the duffle with a pitiful expression. She came closer to me and said, "I want you to know that I'm going to spend the rest of my life being the best mother I can be."

Maybe it was because she sounded so sincere that I believed her and it made me feel good. I knew I should feel more, but this was a start. Just then, the door opened and we went in. The lobby was spacious, with beautiful tiled floors and a large front desk. All the people who worked there had on matching blazers with the hotel logo on their pockets.

I had never stayed at a place like this before. We took an elevator to our floor. Our room was like in a hotel on TV. It had a small living room and a bedroom. My mom, Aunt Celeste, and I would spend the night together. Ms. Terri and Ms. Ann stayed long enough to discuss how the next day would go. They would take us to the airport for an early afternoon flight. Ms. Terri would travel with us, and Ms. Ann gave my mom a phone number for a social worker we had to contact in Philadelphia.

I kept silent while the four of them talked as if I wasn't in the room. I was used to moving around, but I started getting really nervous again. It wasn't because the next day would be the first time I would fly on a plane. I had

always wanted to do that. It wasn't even because I would
be sleeping in another strange bed at the hotel. I was
accustomed to that, and this hotel was better than any
other I'd stayed in. I was in a room with my mom and
my aunt. My dad, grandparents, and cousins were all in
Philadelphia, waiting to meet me. But all of them felt like
strangers. To make matters worse, the one person I loved
the most was already in Philadelphia, facing criminal
charges there.

My stomach spun around. I wanted to be with people
I knew, like my uncle, Felicia, Rachel, and Sabrina. Now
I was scared. This wasn't like being with the Sutlers. I
knew that staying with them was going to be temporary.
But I was about to *live* in Philadelphia. I hadn't lived
anywhere permanently with my uncle. Even when I
thought we had made a home somewhere, it was never
long before we had to leave. All my life, I dreamed what it
would be like to have a mother. Now I did, it scared me.
I didn't know if I was more afraid of her being someone I
wouldn't like or of me being someone she would end up
not liking.

When Ms. Terri and Ms. Ann left, my mom, Aunt
Celeste, and I sat down to eat the dinner that had been
ordered from room service. I learned that my mom was a
fourth-grade teacher and Aunt Celeste was a supervisor
at an insurance company. I was never uneasy around
teachers, but what could it mean that my mom was one,
even if was at an elementary school? Was she going to be
worse than Uncle Kenneth was about making sure my
homework was done? Was she going to make me study
all the time? What about my TV time? My mom went to
the gym twice a week—maybe I'd catch a show then. She
also liked movies and music.

The conversation shifted to my mom and Aunt

Celeste reminiscing. They shared stories about growing up and their school days, but they wouldn't mention Uncle Kenneth at all, so I didn't either. I just laughed at all their funny stories, especially those with my grandmother, my mom's mom. My mom started by saying, "Your grandmother is... how should I say this... uh, *different.*"

Aunt Celeste agreed, but they couldn't seem to find the words to explain how she really was. My grandfather had always been a quiet man, they said. He didn't speak much at all.

Then they asked about me. I told them about Rachel and Felicia, and then I stopped. My mom and aunt already saw Felicia as a hero for calling the police. They hadn't met her, but they wished they had, especially my mom.

They wanted to know what I liked to do. I was careful. I didn't want to say I liked TV, and I knew I couldn't talk about Uncle Kenneth. I wasn't sure what to say, so I told them that I wanted to be a veterinarian. I was feeling more and more nervous. It was like they had to pull things out of me. I guess I was afraid of what they would think of me, especially my mom. I couldn't tell them that I was alone a lot, and how difficult it was, and how many lies Uncle Kenneth had told me. I couldn't go into how much I missed him, either. I kept things as basic as I could. Sometimes they laughed at something I said when it wasn't my intention to be funny. I began to feel a little relaxed, so I talked about my teachers and schoolmates, just like they had. They seemed to enjoy my stories, so I kept going. But then I slipped. I referred to Uncle Kenneth as my dad. It got quiet. It was a mistake. I looked down. My mom leaned toward me.

"It's okay Jasmine. It's not your fault."

But I felt like it was. I know my mom and everybody wanted to find me, but they were living their lives just fine without me. If I had listened to Uncle Kenneth and stayed in the hotel room, I would have never met Felicia, she would have never called the police, and he wouldn't have been sent to jail. I felt like this mess was all my fault. I couldn't hold it in. I cried with my tears landing right on the chicken nuggets and French fries I had barely eaten. My mom jumped up and held me. Aunt Celeste came over and knelt down in front of me. They both kept telling me it was fine.

"Go ahead. Let it out, sweetie," my mom said, and I did. I really did.

"I swear, when I see Kenny..." my mom said.

"You and me both," Aunt Celeste replied. "What the hell was he thinking all these years?"

I was in the bedroom that my mom and I would share, preparing for bed, when I heard her and Aunt Celeste talking. My aunt would sleep on the sofa bed in the living room. As I started to undress in the bedroom, I went to the door and cracked it open.

"Kenny didn't tell Jasmine about any of us," Aunt Celeste said.

"At least he didn't say *you* were dead," my mom said.

"God, were we that bad as a family that he would keep us from her?"

My mom said, "I'm worried about Jasmine, though. She still loves him like he's her father."

"Don't worry, Robin," Aunt Celeste told her. "This is all new for her. Kenny *has* been her dad all her life, for eleven years."

"I know. That's what really tears me up inside." My mom was angry. "I'm so disgusted with Kenny. I would kick his ass if he were here. He didn't even have the decency to do the best with her. She should have had a lot of friends and she only had one, for God's sake, plus the girl from that hotel. She wasn't in any after-school clubs. A girl her age should be able to have fun."

"Well, Terri told us they moved around a lot. How could she make friends?"

"Yeah, and she was by herself too much. I would have never thought Kenny would be like that," my mom said.

It was quiet for a minute. I pressed my ear against the doorway.

"Remember how I was, Celeste?" my mom asked, her voice starting to crack. She reminded my aunt about how finding me was all she thought and talked about. "I couldn't hold onto friends or a man. I know I still have trust issues. I can't even call my own daughter Alexis, the name I gave her. Kenny took that away from me, too."

It was my mom's turn to let it out, and Aunt Celeste comforted her as my mom had me.

"We'll get through this," Aunt Celeste said. "All of us."

Through her tears, my mom managed to say, "I finally have her now, and Kenny won't be in the way to make our recovery difficult."

It hurt me to hear them talk about my uncle like that. I wanted to run out and defend him. He had been my dad my whole life. I wanted to tell them I had plenty of good times with him. So what if I didn't have many friends or wasn't in any clubs? I had Rachel. And Uncle Kenneth did let me see her, a few times at her house and when he was home at our apartment. And I saw her at school. I wanted them to understand that he loved me and cared for me. He was wrong and I still didn't know why he did what he did, but he did do his best with me. That had to count for something. And besides—I loved him.

There were two double beds in the bedroom. I was lying under the covers in one of them when my mom came in. I had left the lamp on, and I watched her take lotion and face cream, deodorant, toothbrush, toothpaste, and some other things out of her bag and put them on the dresser. When Uncle Kenneth and I stayed at hotels, I kept those things in our bags. He always made sure when we left the room that there was nothing out. To make it easier for myself, I never put anything on any tables or dressers. My mom didn't know I was awake until she was ready to go to sleep. She had on a big T-shirt, nothing satiny like I thought moms wore to bed. I surprised her.

"Oh, Jasmine. I didn't know you were up. Are you okay, sweetheart?"

I sat up and asked her if she hated my uncle now.

"Why would you ask me that?"

I shrugged my shoulders.

She looked as if she was choosing her words carefully. It was the same look I had seen on Uncle Kenneth many times. She sat on her bed facing me.

"I really don't know how I feel about him now."

But, she said, Uncle Kenneth had been a great brother to my mom and Aunt Celeste. He had been protective of them.

"He was like another dad to us."

He would chase them when they were little. "He would act like a monster, and we would run around the house screaming." Their parents had to quiet them and sometimes order them to their rooms because they played so loud. The way she told the stories, the three of them seemed to get along so well.

"That's why I don't know how to feel. Can you see what I mean by that?"

"He took care of me," I said flatly.

"I know it seems that way, Jasmine, but your Uncle Kenny wasn't..."

"He did!" I snapped.

My mom looked stunned. She paused and looked away. She bit her lip. Then she nodded and said "okay" so softly, she almost mouthed it.

"We'll talk about it some other time. Why don't you get some sleep," she said.

I turned over angrily. I didn't even say goodnight. She and Aunt Celeste didn't know their brother like they thought they did, and they weren't being fair. After all, they hadn't seen him since I was a baby. He played with me like he had with them. He *did* take care of me, and I wished everyone would realize that I knew him better than they did.

Chapter Eleven

The next morning, I turned over and saw my mom in the other bed, curled up asleep. I got up to look at her. Her face was smooth. Her nails were short and filed, but not manicured by a professional, like Sabrina's were. I could see one of her legs. There was a little scar near her ankle. It looked like something she could have gotten from playing outside. I couldn't deny that I also felt safe with her, as strange as that was. After all, I just met her.

I went over to the TV and turned it on with the volume as low as possible. I clicked through channels to see if there was any update about me. If there was, I sure couldn't catch it.

My mom opened her eyes. With a just-woke-up voice, she asked what I was doing. She didn't think it was a good idea for me to watch the news yet. Of course not. She probably listened to Ms. Ann's advice on how to handle me. She sat up and asked me to sit next to her. She had a little crust around her eyes, but that didn't take away how pretty she was.

"Jasmine, I want to apologize for making you upset last night. I know how hard it's been for you. I'm going to try to make it easier. I guess there's a lot for both of us to learn."

I didn't know what to say. I just nodded my head. I was still angry, although I was glad she said she was sorry.

My mom didn't push me for a response. She just went to the bathroom to wash. While she was there, I realized that I had not called my mom anything yet. I wasn't sure what to call her. I wasn't used to saying "Mom," and I wasn't sure I was ready to call her that anyway. "Ms. Robin" sounded so formal. So far, I hadn't had a reason to call her by name. She was always close to me, so I could tap her on her arm to get her attention. I wondered, while she was in the shower that morning, if I should say something to her. I said aloud to myself, "Mom, can I watch television?" to see how it would feel. It was weird. It was definitely something I would have to get used to.

"All yours," my mom said as she returned from the bathroom. Then she opened her suitcase and pulled out clothes that were neatly folded and paired, a shirt and pants. Uncle Kenneth didn't care about how I packed my clothes. We rushed so often that I just stuffed clothes into the bags. While I was in the bathroom, as the water flowed from the faucet, I remembered all the places I had lived or stayed. There were a lot. I was hoping that it would be awhile before I stayed at another hotel.

From outside the door, my mom asked me what I was wearing. I had no idea and didn't expect the question—Uncle Kenneth would only say I couldn't wear something if it was too tight or "too adult." I hadn't pulled anything out of my duffle bag. As I went through my bags, clothes awfully wrinkled, she pointed out that we needed to go shopping. That was just what I wanted to hear her say—but it wouldn't happen until we were in Philadelphia. But I had something to look forward to, at least.

After we all had ordered breakfast in the room, Ms. Terri and Ms. Ann met us at the hotel and drove us to the airport. Although no one really talked about him, I found out that my uncle would be going to court soon for an arraignment—an appearance before a judge. Although my mom had said it was okay to have those feelings, I still didn't feel comfortable telling anyone that I was worried about him or that I was thinking about him. I didn't want to hurt her or make her and Aunt Celeste angrier than they already were. But I knew Uncle Kenneth had to be scared and I knew he missed me. I wondered if they would let me see him if I asked. Now wasn't the time, but I decided that when we got settled, I would ask.

It was time to say goodbye to Ms. Ann. When she embraced me, she told me she was confident that I would do well. Ms. Ann gave my mom her phone number and references for counselors. She said the court would likely require family therapy. There were programs I watched on television where people saw psychiatrists. Was that the kind of counselor I would have to see? I didn't think I needed one. My mom and I were getting along so far. Sure, it had been really crazy lately, but did I need to see someone about it? I thought I had been strong, considering what had just happened. But I supposed they had already made the decision for me, and it wouldn't be too long before I would meet with a therapist. But I didn't want to think about that. I would fly on a plane for the first time soon. Uncle Kenneth had promised that he would take me to Disney World on a plane. I couldn't tell anyone, especially my mom, about that promise or that I wished he was with me. Did he think the same thing when *he* flew to Philadelphia? Did he even get a chance to see how pretty the sky was?

My mom gave me the window seat and I stared out of it the entire flight. It was thrilling to watch the ground fall away beneath us. The world was so small when we reached the sky. Sometimes the sun was so bright I had to close my eyes. Other times, the clouds looked like huge, soft pillows. And for a little while I felt far away from where I was going now, from all the cities I had lived in, from all the hotels I had stayed in. I didn't feel like I was anywhere or I belonged to anyone. I felt calmer than I had in a while, but it was a short flight, and before I knew it, the plane's wheels hit the ground again, in Philadelphia. My stomach started to turn. My mom, Aunt Celeste, Ms. Terri, and I were the last to leave the plane. Ms. Terri warned us that there were reporters in the airport, as we thought there might be.

My mom signaled Aunt Celeste, who, I was told, was prepared to talk to them with Ms. Terri, while my mom and I met Uncle Malcolm in a different part of the airport. It was incredible that there were so many people who wanted to know about me. Ms. Terri walked ahead of us. My mom gave me a baseball cap to wear and told me to pull the brim way down. She shielded me as much as she could while people shoved microphones at us. Camera lights flashed over and over again. People shouted questions at us, just as they had when I arrived at the police station with Ms. Terri. She and Aunt Celeste drew most of them away from us, but there were a determined few who moved in our direction. Police officers blocked them from coming any closer. I couldn't hear my aunt's and Ms. Terri's comments—there was so much noise. My mom and I stayed close to a pair of plainclothes officers. My mom kept me close, and I leaned close to her until we reached the airport police station. Uncle Malcolm's car was parked right outside. He was leaning against it, and his face lit up when he saw us. He hugged my mom and she said, "This is Jasmine."

"Well, it's nice to meet you, Jasmine," he said, and put his hand out to shake mine.

I said hello and shook his large hand. Uncle Malcolm was a burly man, tall, with broad shoulders and a round belly. He opened the back door of the car for us, and my mom and I sat next to each other.

"I'll be glad when this dies down," my mom said. I agreed. I didn't like that there were so many people around me almost every time I went outside. I had gone from living with my uncle, who didn't want anyone to know us, to strangers wanting to know everything about me. I'd seen the news so many times before and I had watched celebrities give interviews, and now I was the one on TV. Well, not me exactly. No one had really seen my face, but they sure knew about me. I wanted to know why everyone was so interested.

"They're interested because our story is not something you hear every day, but don't worry, sweetheart, it'll all end soon," my mom reassured me. While Uncle Malcolm drove, I rested my head on the back of the seat. My hand landed on a crayon. I suspected it was my cousin's. I hadn't had much time to think about them. I'm the oldest cousin. What did that really mean? Would they look up to me like I had to Felicia? I hadn't been around many young kids. In fact, Melanie at the Sutlers' house was the most time I'd spent with a small child. Uncle Kenneth didn't have any friends, at least none that I was aware of, so we never went to the houses of his co-workers, who might have had kids. Rachel had a younger brother, but she and I always kicked him out of her bedroom. I still missed being with Rachel. I was worried that I wouldn't find friends like her and Felicia. I wished I could have talked to them. I was sure they'd seen me—well, news of me—on TV. I wasn't sure if Felicia was interested. I hoped Sabrina would help her. I really thought Felicia was upset that I now had my mom, and she didn't have hers. That made me sad. I thought maybe my mom would let me call her and Rachel.

My mom bombarded Uncle Malcolm with questions about what was happening with the news reports. Her voice rose when he told her that everyone was talking to the press. Family members my mom and aunt hadn't seen or talked to in years were doing interviews. My real dad hadn't talked to reporters, but he also had family who *were* talking.

But Uncle Malcolm saved the best—or worst—for last.

"She what?" my mom yelled when Uncle Malcolm told us that my grandmother had given an exclusive interview to one of the local television reporters just that morning. Her yell startled me. I was glad neither of them saw me shake. I was feeling very jumpy. I felt nervous—I hadn't sleep well.

Uncle Malcolm said he was there for the interview. He had tried to talk my grandmother out of it. "You know how she is, Robin, when an idea pops in her head," he said. "I don't know what will come of this. It was real bad." he added. My mom looked worried. "You'll get to see it. It's coming on tonight's news."

I hoped that I could watch it, but I figured I wouldn't ask my mom if I could see it until it was almost time for the news to come on.

I stared out the car window at the summer early evening. I looked at the highway signs. I used to do that all the time with Uncle Kenneth. But unlike any other time, I didn't have to wonder where we going or where we would stay for the night. I wished I could talk to him. He knew his family better than I did, except for Uncle Malcolm. Uncle Kenneth could have told me what to expect and how I should be with them. But then again,

I knew my uncle. He would have urged me to be myself. Funny thing was, I felt like I had to figure that out all over again—who I was. I wasn't sure I knew.

The ride to my mom's house was smooth—there wasn't much traffic. When we left the highway, I looked at houses and wondered if my mom's was anything like those we passed. Then we slowed down and turned onto a block of row homes and stopped, because plainclothes officers and Ms. Terri had parked their cars in the middle of the street. There was activity in front of one house. My mom leaned forward to get a clearer view. Ms. Terri came to our car to tell us the media was there. They were talking to neighbors about my mom. Ms. Terri told us to wait until the officers directed them off the block. Aunt Celeste, who rode to the house with Ms. Terri, came out to the car and got into the front seat, next to Uncle Malcolm. I looked at the block. There were people outside and TV reporters in front of one of their neighbors' homes. The neighbors had noticed me in the back of the car, and they peered at me like I was an exhibit in a museum. They pointed and talked. I ducked down in the seat. Ms. Terri and the plainclothes officers finally moved the reporters away. Uncle Malcolm pulled into a parking space in front of my mom's house. As soon as we stepped to the curb, two of my mom's neighbors started to approach us. They were black and looked like they were Ms. Baxter's age.

"Here come the nosy ones who just can't wait until we even reach the first step," Aunt Celeste said. She and my mom stood on either side of me, like I was a princess being protected from kidnappers.

"Hello, Robin. Is that Alexis?" I heard one of the women say.

"Yes, that's Jasmine," my mom said to the woman.

Ms. Terri told the women that the family needed to get settled.

"We understand," the other woman said and added, "Maybe tomorrow?"

My mom didn't answer her. The plainclothes officers started to escort them away. I heard one of them snap, "You don't have to touch me. I'm just a concerned neighbor."

The officers stood outside the house while we went up the front steps. I still had the baseball cap on and I kept my head down.

My mom looked at me for approval when we entered the house. It was much smaller than the Sutlers' house, but larger than any place Uncle Kenneth and I had lived in. There were figurines on the end tables, paintings on the walls. She had nice wooden floors, with an oval rug in the living room.

"Let me show you around," she said, grabbing my hand. The dining room was painted a nice burnt-orange color. "Excuse the table," she said. There were papers everywhere. Maybe she had been rushing when she left and didn't have time to clean up. The kitchen was too small to have a full table in it, but there was a counter and two stools under it. There was an opening in the kitchen wall so that you could see into the dining room. There were no dishes on the counter, and there was a dishwasher. My mom opened the back door to a backyard with a grill and two big plants on the porch. The basement had a washer and dryer and a shelf full of school things—paper, binders, folders, markers, and construction paper.

"I use a lot of this stuff to decorate my classroom," my mom explained.

I didn't say anything during my tour, but I liked my

mom's house. She had saved the best for the end. She showed me my room. My mouth dropped. She said she had painted it as soon as she moved in a year ago, before she even painted her own bedroom. She kept thinking one day she'd have me back, and she wanted to be ready for me. She thought about what color a teenage girl might like. It was lavender. She said, "Now, we don't have to stay with this color. We can repaint it whatever color you want."

The room had a dresser, a desk, and a bed already made up with sheets. I never had a room as nice as this one. Uncle Kenneth got me the basics, but all of the furniture came from second-hand stores. Everything was new in this bedroom.

"Go ahead. Sit on your bed." My mom smiled and watched my every move. I could tell she was fighting back tears. I sat on the bed. It felt better than any other I'd had.

"You did all this for me, even before you knew where I was?"

"Your Aunt Celeste and your grandmother thought I was crazy. Even your dad thought I shouldn't have done this. But I just wanted to, and I'm glad I did." She told me she would sit in the room by herself sometimes and pretend I was there. "I wouldn't tell anyone about that. They would really think I was out of my mind," she said, as she looked around my bedroom. She suggested I spend some time alone in my new room. "You come downstairs when you're ready."

"Can I watch the news tonight?" I blurted out as she began to leave.

She turned and looked at me. "I don't know, Jasmine. Why would you want to?"

"Please," I whispered. "I'll be okay."

She exhaled and agreed, but said she would turn it off if she saw any sign of me getting upset. She kissed me on the forehead and left.

I walked around my bedroom. I opened the sliding closet doors and looked at the empty space. I put my duffle bag in it. I sat at the desk to see what it would feel like to do my homework there. With Uncle Kenneth, I studied at the kitchen table. Usually, when he wasn't there, I did my homework with the television on. I doubted that my mom would allow that. The walls were bare, which I liked. When we ran from home the last time, Uncle Kenneth made me leave my posters behind.

Then I thought of Uncle Kenneth. I began to feel guilty. There I was in a new bedroom, thinking about how I would decorate it, and he was in a jail cell. *What was he doing right then? Was he afraid? Did he have anybody to talk to? When would he have his own bedroom to decorate the way he wanted?* He had made so many sacrifices for me, and now he had nothing. I didn't stay in the room much longer. I couldn't.

When I went back downstairs, Aunt Celeste and Uncle Malcolm had ordered pizza for dinner. My mom was checking her voicemail. It was nice she had a phone in her house. Uncle Kenneth had cell phones only, and he replaced them each time we moved. As my mom listened to her messages, I sat on the couch and found myself trying not to enjoy my surroundings. It just didn't seem fair. If I knew Uncle Kenneth was in a safe, nice place, then maybe I would have felt better. But the thought of him in prison just made me sick and unable to feel good about anything.

"I've never had so many messages," my mom said as she sat down on the couch beside me. She said that Ms. Ann had already called to see how I was and that she had a surprise for me. "Your dad is coming over tomorrow to meet you." I looked at her sharply. I wasn't ready for that yet. I wasn't thrilled to meet him. In my mind, I already had a dad.

"Now don't get nervous," she said. "It's going to be fine. Like I said, he really can't wait to meet you."

It was my fault. Ms. Ann had asked me at the Sutlers' if I wanted to see my real dad. I had lied and said yes. Ms. Terri had asked me again at the hotel, and I said yes again. It was easy to withhold the truth. But now I had only a little time to get myself together. I would have to act as I had so many times before with Uncle Kenneth. I convinced myself I could do it again. At least I hoped I could.

"So, are you excited? He sure is. Almost half those messages were from him."

"I'm excited to see him, too," I lied. My mom was so cheerful. It just seemed easier to pretend that I was eager to meet him. If she was that pleased, he was probably was, too. I didn't want to hurt anybody, but I couldn't help how I felt. The longer I was away from Uncle Kenneth, the more I missed him, and the more I missed him, the more I wondered if I had done the right thing by being friends with Felicia. All of this was because I had trusted her.

Luckily, for the rest of the evening, I didn't have to discuss my real dad. The big topic was my grandmother, who had called to speak to me before the evening news.

"Hello, Jasmine. This is your grandmother, Doreen. But of course you won't call me that. You can call me Grandmom, Nana, Granny, Mom-Mom, anything you want, except Doreen, okay?" She said it all before I even said hi.

I just answered, "Okay." She had a playful voice, like

a character on a kids' TV show. She went on to say she couldn't wait to meet me, that she had planned a special dinner for the whole family, and that my grandfather wanted to talk to me, but he was in the bathroom. I just sat silently with the phone.

Then my mom then grabbed the phone from me, while my grandmother was in mid-sentence, and said, "Mom... Mom...." Then she shouted, "Mom! We have to go. Jasmine will talk to you later."

I could hear my grandmother's voice on the other end. My mom said yes a few times, saying that we would watch the news program. My mom didn't mention how upset she was about the interview.

The TV interview with my grandmother was okay. I thought Uncle Malcolm had exaggerated how bad it was. He and my Aunt Celeste joked about my grandmother's wig being a little crooked. I had to admit, my grandmother didn't have to reveal how young my mom was when she had me, and no, I'm sure Uncle Kenneth wouldn't want people to know that he was actually nerdy growing up and that my grandmother still couldn't believe that he had the confidence to raise me. The interview at the airport with Aunt Celeste wasn't as smooth. She had snarled at a reporter and asked if he got his journalism degree at a paper goods store, just because he had probed a little too much.

My mom turned to Aunt Celeste sharply.

"I didn't think they would put that on the air," Aunt Celeste said. "Look, he went too far."

"You are no longer the family spokesperson," my mom snapped.

Chapter Twelve

The next morning I was awakened by the phone and doorbell ringing nonstop. I couldn't go back to sleep. After a few of the phone calls, my mom knocked on my door to wake me up. She was already dressed and in a really good mood. She brought in my clothes, which she had washed the night before. She suggested what I should wear and volunteered to curl my hair a little differently. She even lent me one of her bracelets to dress up my outfit. I enjoyed the attention. I rummaged through her jewelry box in her bedroom, which was fun. She must have already felt comfortable with me, because her bedroom wasn't neat like the rest of the house. She didn't even attempt to move shirts off her chair, papers were spread across her dresser, and several pairs of shoes were tossed in different places on the floor. She didn't apologize for it, either.

Uncle Kenneth wasn't like that. He was incredibly neat, and not just at the hotels where we stayed. He made sure we kept things in their places at home as well. It never occurred to me that it was his tactic to save time packing whenever we had to leave suddenly. My mom didn't have to worry about rushing to pack until she got the call that I had been found. Her room looked like that's what had happened. Her bathroom was no better. Her towel and washcloth were thrown over her rack. An opened bag of cotton balls was on the counter, as well as nail polish, nail polish remover, and a comb. It wasn't what I imagined her rooms would look like. I don't know why, but I thought my mom would be really organized.

In the midst of her mess, she did a good job in dressing me up and she knew how to style hair. I could tell she was happy. After all, it was an important day for her. I was too caught up in her hands caressing my hair as she curled it, and in laughing as we talked, to even think about how significant the day really was.

Then the bell rang again. Reality struck.

We went downstairs, and my mom opened the door to a woman who had had to walk past the reporters who were on the sidewalk in front of our house. My mom told them she had no comment. I knew instantly that this woman was another social worker. She had the same professional look as Ms. Ann, and she had a thick folder like Ms. Ann always had. Her name was Mrs. Samuels. She was older than my mom, but not Mrs. Sutler's age. She was black, too, and pleasant, but I wouldn't have expected her to be any other way.

I was prepared to have more of what adults call "small talk" while I ate breakfast, but Mrs. Samuels seemed to have something else in mind. She really wanted to know how I felt at that very moment, not replay what had happened. She paid close attention to me when my mom brought up my real dad in the conversation.

He would be at the house soon. I felt unsettled again and I thought Mrs. Samuels sensed it. She asked if I was ready to meet my dad. I still didn't want to admit to what she probably already knew. Besides, I didn't want to crush my mom's feelings—she was more thrilled than she was the night before.

The truth was that I couldn't get Uncle Kenneth out

of my mind. I thought about him all the time, including when my real dad suddenly came through the door.

Mrs. Samuels jumped up at the same time I did. She followed me into the living room. My dad had a huge smile on his face. He was a big man, like Uncle Malcolm, and about an inch or two taller than my mom. He looked just like the picture on my mom's cell phone—bald head, neat mustache and beard. Before he even said a word, my mom began crying.

He seemed nice. He greeted me excitedly. I said hi, but with less emotion. He gave me a gift. By then, Mrs. Samuels was standing next to me. I didn't say much. I thanked him, and again I felt like I was on stage with everyone watching me. I pulled the wrapping paper off the box. Inside was a blank journal and a really nice, thick book about animals.

"Your mother told me you want to be a veterinarian."

Who told her to do that? I thought.

"And," he continued, "since everything is so new for you, maybe you could write down how you feel."

I was quiet for a second.

"Isn't that a nice gift?" my mom asked.

I nodded my head and thanked him. I could barely look at him. It was quiet again.

He glanced at my mom, back at me, and then said, "I was also thinking that after you get settled, we could all go to the zoo. They have a lot of different programs and you could join one. You know, to learn more about animals."

I nodded my head again and put the box down on the coffee table.

My mom spoke after few seconds of silence. "Jasmine, what's wrong, I thought you'd be happy to...."

Mrs. Samuels cut her off by placing her index finger to her lips and shaking her head.

I was supposed to say something. I was supposed to jump up in my dad's arms and kiss his cheeks. I was supposed to cry with delight at seeing him for the first time. I knew that's what I was probably supposed to do, but instead, I ran up the steps to my bedroom, closed the door, and fell on the bed. It was too much. I knew I hurt my dad, and that made me feel even worse. But he didn't feel like my dad—he felt like a stranger.

No surprise, there was a knock at the door. It was my mom and Mrs. Samuels. I didn't talk. I just opened the door and sat on the side of the bed. I looked at the design on the rug.

"What's wrong, baby?" my mom asked. "Aren't you happy to see your dad?"

"Um, Robin, do you mind if you leave us alone for a minute?" Mrs. Samuels asked quietly.

Without looking up at her, I knew my mom didn't like it, but she agreed. Mrs. Samuels sat down next to me. She asked me if I missed my uncle. I figured she knew the answer before I told her. Didn't everyone else? Uncle Kenneth had been my dad my whole life.

"They've been hoping to have you back for a long time and they're ready to make you a part of their family. Maybe overly ready, but ready nonetheless," Mrs. Samuels said.

I could understand that, but *what about my uncle?* "No one even says his name. *I* can't even say his name," I said.

She explained the anger my family, especially my mom, felt about Uncle Kenneth.

"He took you away from them, took away their chance to know you like he does, their chance to watch you grow and change, their chance to call you by your birth name. They feel that he stole you from them."

"My mom and dad gave me up," I snapped. "They just handed me over to him. I don't have a baby, but if I did, I'd never do that. Now they're here with me and he's in jail."

Mrs. Samuels asked me if I knew why my parents let me go.

"I know about what they agreed. My mom probably wanted it because I would have gotten in the way of her making friends in school or going on dates. And my dad was in college doing his own thing."

Mrs. Samuels shook her head and replied, "You have to remember, Jasmine, when your mother was your age she may have been less mature than you and very scared. Your Uncle Kenneth was an adult. He was twenty-one when your mother had you."

I didn't like where Mrs. Samuels was taking the conversation. I was uncomfortable. I said, "He was only a couple of years older than my dad."

"Your mother and your aunt looked up to him. Could it be that *he* convinced *them* that giving you to him was the best thing to do?"

"No! My dad, I mean, Uncle Kenneth, wouldn't do that. He wouldn't try to make my mom give up her own child." I was obviously the only person who really knew Uncle Kenneth.

"Why are you so sure?" Mrs. Samuels was calm.

"Because I just know he wouldn't."

"Just like you knew your Uncle Kenneth was your father? Just like you knew that he was the only family you had? And just like you knew without a shadow of a doubt that you didn't have a mother?"

"That's different," I snapped again.

"Why?" she asked.

"Because... because... it just is."

Mrs. Samuels remained silent. I knew she wanted me to think, in the same way Felicia had when Sabrina told us about the flyer of me at the supermarket. I looked away.

Mrs. Samuels stood and told me that I didn't need to go back downstairs until I was ready. She also said she would be coming every day to see me. When she closed the door behind her, I fell back on the bed. Shortly after that, the front door downstairs opened and closed, and then I heard muffled words from my mom and Mrs. Samuels. My dad must have left. I turned on my side. I really wished I hadn't hurt him, but I knew Uncle Kenneth was hurt, too. Why was I the only one who cared about that? Have they forgotten the sacrifices he made? *He* raised a child that wasn't even *his*.

I hadn't realized that I had fallen asleep, until a light knock on the door made me open my eyes. I didn't even know what time it was.

"Jasmine?" It was my mom. "Can I come in?"

I told her yes. She wanted to check on me and apologize. She seemed to have been doing a lot of that lately. She didn't mean to push me in any direction, she said. I figured Mrs. Samuels did some talking with her while I was asleep. My mom told me that I would be starting therapy the following week and Mrs. Samuels thought it might be a good idea for me to see my uncle.

I sat up. I started smiling, to my mom's dismay.

"Really?" I asked. I wanted to know when. It had to be arranged, but it wouldn't happen until after a few therapy sessions. I didn't mind. My mood instantly changed. I was feeling happier than I had since Uncle Kenneth was arrested.

"You're excited about seeing your Uncle Kenny, huh?" my mom asked softly.

She didn't understand. It was all I had wanted since the last time I saw him. I needed to tell him that I heard him yell that he loved me when the officer was taking him away. I had to let him know that I wasn't mad at him and I missed him so much.

I told my mom I was glad that I would be seeing Uncle Kenneth and I asked if she had talked to him.

She quietly said, "Not yet," and then quickly changed the subject.

She had prepared some food and wanted me to eat. I got up. I now felt like I could eat a big meal. I was so excited. As my mom and I were about to go downstairs, she turned and saw my duffle bag stuffed with my clothes on the closet floor. I had forgotten to close the closet door.

"You put your things back in your bag, Jasmine?"

After getting dressed, I put my other clothes back in there. I didn't feel comfortable putting them in the drawers. Where were Uncle Kenneth's clothes? He didn't have a dresser and a closet.

"This is your home," she said. "You can unpack now."

"I know. I, um, I..." I couldn't think of anything to say. I kept the real reason to myself.

"Are you afraid that you'll have to move again?"

That sounded good to me, so I went along with it. My mom hugged me and promised that if we were to move, it wouldn't be for a long while.

"This is your home," she repeated. "So you can start unpacking tonight."

After dinner that night, I unpacked. Every piece of clothing reminded me of Uncle Kenneth.

Chapter Thirteen

My mom is not a bad cook. That evening was the first time we ate alone together. She turned off the house phone and her cell phone, and the doorbell rang but she ignored it while we ate. Reporters were still calling and stopping by, attempting to schedule interviews with her and me. She wasn't interested and she refused to allow my grandmother or Aunt Celeste to give interviews, either. While we ate, we stayed away from the topics of my my dad or Uncle Kenneth. That seemed to help us get through the meal without any tension.

We talked about the upcoming weekend. On Sunday, we were going to my grandparents' house for the family dinner my grandmother was preparing. Apparently, I had a large family. But my mom told me that all of them wouldn't be at the dinner. We laughed as she described some of our relatives. Then someone suddenly pounded on the front door. Both of us jumped. My mom went to the door, peeked through the window, and opened it excitedly.

"What are you guys doing here? And what's wrong with you, scaring me like that?" my mom said, laughing, as a woman and two men entered. They were just as thrilled to see her as she was to see them. My mom introduced Ms. Michelle, Mr. Gary, and Mr. Shane to me. They were her friends. My mom had already talked about them.

Ms. Michelle told my mom the gym wasn't as fun without her.

My mom beamed and explained that she'd be back after I was settled.

As they talked, I noticed Mr. Shane. He stared at my mom like Felicia had with Ricky. In fact, after all the introductions, Mr. Shane offered to help my mom bring in some drinks for us. They were in the kitchen longer than I thought it took to pour iced tea in five glasses. Her other friends kept talking to me. I suspected it was to keep me from noticing how long my mom and Mr. Shane were out of the room.

It was fine. My mom's friends were funny and I could see myself having no problem getting along with them. They were nice enough not to ask me anything that would make me uneasy. Instead, they shared funny stories about things that happened between them and my mom.

I learned that my mom knew Ms. Michelle first. She said it was a struggle to get my mom to join them for anything. "She stayed home all the time. I had to almost drag her out of the house just to see a movie with us."

But all of them had been patient. They knew about me and knew about how my mom missed me and had wanted to help find me.

"So, is Mr. Shane your boyfriend?" I asked my mom after her friends left.

"Why do you ask that?" She blushed.

"You two seem closer than the others." They not only spent more than just a few minutes alone together, he also stayed a little longer than the other two. But he didn't go too far with asking me questions. He let my mom lead the conversation. I was more relaxed with Mr.

Shane, meeting him for the first time, than I was with my dad.

"Well, he's not my boyfriend, although he would like to be," my mom said.

"Do *you* want him to be?"

"I don't know. It's not a good time."

"If you say so," I said.

In bed that night, I thought about my mom and her friends. I realized for the first time how my mom's life must have been before I arrived, and it seemed better than Uncle Kenneth's. My mom had her sister, her parents, and her friends. She had a man who wanted to be with her. Uncle Kenneth had none of that. He only had me. I never saw him with friends. *I* was his friend. He didn't join a gym or a sports team. Didn't he ever feel like he missed out on things? Didn't he want to fall in love and have a girlfriend? Was I ever in his way? I didn't seem to be. He never seemed tired of having me around him. He always found new things for us to do together. Growing up, I had been angry that Uncle Kenneth kept me so close to him, but as I lay in bed that night, it seemed strange to me that he *chose* to have a life with only me in it.

Chapter Fourteen

I had to buy some new things to wear, which my mom and I did that Saturday. Aunt Celeste joined us, just in case she had to keep someone from approaching us. A few reporters did follow us for a little while, but we managed to lose them at a stop light. They still wanted comments even after my mom decided, with Mrs. Samuels' help, to agree to one interview with a local TV news reporter. My mom thought that if she did one, then maybe the calls and the visits would stop. Mrs. Samuels knew the reporter, which made my mom more relaxed.

My mom was great. She was pretty and she answered the questions smoothly. It helped that the reporter promised to stay away from certain subjects. The interview was in our living room and it didn't take too long, either.

No sooner had it aired than my mom was on the phone and answering text messages like she was a celebrity. The visits from reporters did slow down, but didn't exactly stop.

"I don't like that on her," Aunt Celeste said about a summer dress I paraded in the dressing room. She thought it was too short. My mom wasn't that fond of it either, but she bought it for me because I liked it. Then Aunt Celeste said one of the tops I picked out was too low. I begged and pleaded until my mom got that one, too. She said she could pin it to make it less revealing.

After I tried on jeans that Aunt Celeste thought were

too tight, I heard her whisper to my mom, "You can't let her have everything she wants, Robin."

"I know," she said, but she didn't say no to me all afternoon. And as a surprise, my mom made a hair appointment for me and she let me have a manicure. By the time we went to my grandparents' house on Sunday, I felt prettier than ever before. Aunt Celeste even approved of my dress. With Uncle Kenneth, the only time I dressed up was when I graduated from middle school. That was the last time I felt so good about how I looked. I felt special for the dinner. I asked my mom if my real dad would be there. She said no and didn't say anything else. So I stayed on the topic she chose for the rest of the ride in my mom's car. Her car was newer and nicer than any car Uncle Kenneth had. He would change cars often, and I thought it was because they needed constant repair. As I sat in my mom's car, I realized that Uncle Kenneth changed cars to keep us a secret. I didn't share that with my mom. She got tenser the closer we reached my grandparents' house.

Their block was wider than my mom's, with trees and twin houses. It was a quiet street, and I wondered if it was that peaceful when my mom lived there. She, my aunt, and uncle were raised in that house. I would fantasize with Uncle Kenneth about homes like those on the block. I couldn't see my grandparents' house at first because there were so many cars parked along both sides of the street. That was unusual, my mom said.

As my mom was parking, Aunt Celeste called her on her cell phone to tell her about all the people at my grandmother's house. Against my mom's wishes, my grandmother had not only invited many relatives, but there were friends of the family at the house as well. My mom tried to remain calm, but it was obvious she was furious. I could tell she wasn't sure what to do.

"I don't mind going in," I said to her, even though I felt nervous. She smiled and looked at me.

"I'm not sure about that, Jasmine. It may be too overwhelming for you." *She* was the one acting like if she had the chance, she would run away from her parents' block, never to return again.

I actually wanted to meet them. I convinced my mom that I was fine. She decided we would stay for as long as I could take it. The closer we got to the house, though, the more annoyed my mom became.

"They're here!" someone yelled, from among the many people waiting in front of the house. Everyone turned in our direction. We walked up the steps and people gathered around and hugged and kissed us.

People held up their cell phones and took pictures. As a reflex, my mom shielded me as she shouted, "No pictures!"

Then Aunt Celeste chimed in and threatened to take anybody's phone and break it to bits if another photo was taken.

My mom held my hand so tight, it started to ache. She wouldn't let go, even when she was in the house. Then a loud request came from Aunt Celeste, who told the group to step aside. No sooner had I entered the living room when I was grabbed and hugged as a collective "Awww" echoed around us. Then I was kissed repeatedly without me even knowing it was my grandmother who was kissing me. It took my mom and Aunt Celeste to almost pull her off me.

"All right, Mom," Aunt Celeste yelled, "Let the girl breathe!"

Then I could take a look at my grandmother. Her face matched her playful voice. That's not to say she looked silly—she was just pleasant. I didn't know why she wore the wig on TV—her hair, with streaks of gray, was styled fine, pulled back in a bun. She wasn't all that tall, so my mom, aunt, and uncle's height had come from my grandfather, who was standing behind my grandmother. He was a big man. My grandmother couldn't stop smiling and crying.

Again, I felt like I was on stage. Everyone watched our encounter. My grandfather said, "Welcome home, Jasmine," followed by his own hug. Everyone really melted after that.

Then my grandmother grabbed my hand and my grandfather's hand to direct us upstairs. She yelled for everyone, who still stared at us as if they were watching a movie, to go back to whatever they had been doing.

"Mom, where are you taking her?" my mom shouted, as she started to follow us.

"Oh, you just go get something to eat. Jasmine needs some grandparent time." I turned back to my mom. She stood at the bottom of the steps with a anxious expression, like she was afraid I would disappear again.

We went into my grandparents' bedroom. It had a large bed, two dressers, and two separate closets. The bed was made and everything was put away except some bottles, brushes, combs, perfumes, and colognes on one dresser. My grandfather went to a recliner that was in the corner of the room.

"Well, Jasmine," my grandmother started as we sat on the bed next to each other. "I wanted you to have a chance to talk to us for a few minutes and ask us anything you want to know about us, or your mother, or… anything." She was so cheery—really different from my mom and Aunt Celeste and… Uncle Kenneth.

"I don't have any questions right now," I said, and felt bad about it. I didn't want to disappoint them.

My grandmother put her arm around me and squeezed tight. "Oh, that's all right. But know that you can call me or your grandfather any time you want." We both looked at him. He simply smiled.

"So how do you like Philadelphia so far?" she asked.

"It's nice." I didn't know what to say. It didn't feel like home yet.

"I love that dress you have on. You are so pretty. Isn't she pretty, Howard?" We both looked at him again.

My grandfather leaned forward, studied me, and said, "Oh, yeah, she's very pretty."

My grandmother asked me to stand up. "And you're tall, just like your mother was. Doesn't she look just like Robin when she was Jasmine's age?"

My grandfather nodded. "Yeah, she does look just like Robin."

"And you're quiet like her, too, not like your Aunt Celeste. Isn't she just sweet, Howard?"

My grandfather said, "Yes, she is."

My grandmother rolled her eyes at him. I remembered my mom and Aunt Celeste telling me how quiet my grandfather could be. But it didn't seem like he wasn't interested in *me*. He just didn't seem to be interested in this "grandparent time."

"So, are you *sure* you don't have anything to ask us?" my grandmother asked.

I said no.

"Nothing?" she asked again. "Are you really sure?" she practically sang the question.

"All right, Doreen, leave the child alone. You're putting her on the spot. She doesn't have any questions." That was the most my grandfather had said in one breath.

"I'm not putting her on the spot. Am I putting you on the spot, Jasmine?"

Before I could answer, my grandfather replied, "Don't put her on the spot by *asking* her if you're putting her on the spot."

"Well, you won't let our granddaughter speak for herself."

"It's better than forcing her to say something when she has nothing to say."

They went back and forth like that while I sat there. I didn't know what to do. I couldn't leave—that would be rude. I didn't want to interrupt them. What would I say? So, I carefully shifted on the bed, thinking if I moved, they would notice, and remember why we were in the room in the first place. It worked. My grandfather jumped up while my grandmother was in the middle of a sentence.

He stood next to me and said, "Jasmine, I'm your grand-pop, at least that's what your cousins call me. You're free to call me whatever makes you feel comfortable. You can also ask me anything you want, when you're ready. I know it's been hard for you, so I won't push. Now, c'mon. It's time to eat."

And that was that. He took my hand gently and we walked to the door. He turned to my grandmother. "Now stop pouting, Doreen, and join us downstairs."

As soon as I returned to the living room with my grandfather, my mom came running to me and hugged me like she had just found me again.

"Well, she looks like she survived it without any scars," Aunt Celeste said and chuckled as she walked by.

Others came up to me and introduced themselves. Names were thrown at me with such speed, there's was no way I could remember them all. I had great uncles, great aunts, and second and third cousins.

My mom told me not to worry. "Most of these people you won't see again for years," she whispered. I had hoped that it was true for one of my cousins. He was lanky and when he hugged me, I smelled marijuana on his shirt. I used to get a whiff of it from classmates on my way to school.

"Damn, girl, you look just like your mom when she was little."

"The last time he saw me," my mom whispered sarcastically. I struggled to keep from laughing.

He introduced his girlfriend, who looked like she had just puffed on a joint, to us. My mom moved us quickly aside.

"Knowing your grandmother, she probably created a chart for you with everyone's names," she told me. That actually sounded like a good idea.

My face began to ache from smiling so much. As I hugged and greeted all of these new relatives, I felt a small hand slip into mine. I looked down, and a little girl was looking up at me, smiling. She whispered, "Hi." I said hi back. She wouldn't let go of my hand, so I had to use my one free arm to hug the few remaining relatives I was introduced to.

My mom called me into the dining room to sit down. She fixed me a plate with a little bit of everything. The little girl still held my hand. Aunt Celeste came over to us.

"Keisha, let Jasmine eat in peace." I was then formally introduced to my little cousin. I met her brother, Nathan, on different terms. I jumped when I sat down. I didn't expect the head of a Barbie doll to be on my chair. That was how I first met Nathan, who put it there. He made his sister cry—it was from Keisha's Barbie—and Uncle Malcolm had to discipline him in front of everyone. Nathan ended up sitting by himself for a little while.

After that commotion, I began eating dinner across from two great aunts, my grandmother's sisters, who watched every forkful I ate. They marveled at how much I resembled my mom, who sat next to me. They also complimented my grandmother on her interview.

"You looked great," one aunt said.

"Kept that reporter on his toes," the other one replied.

I peeped at my mom, who frowned and bit her lip, then got up to refill my glass. My grandmother glowed at the attention. And then one of my great aunts asked if my grandmother had spoken to Uncle Kenneth.

She had. I remained as cool as I could and kept eating. My grandmother whispered that she had to be quick because my mom didn't want anyone to talk about him, especially in front of me. But my grandmother kept talking right in front of me. Just the thought that someone had recently spoken to Uncle Kenneth made my heart beat faster. I looked at her. She acted like I wasn't there and whispered. My great aunts leaned in closer.

"He apologized to me and Howard. Oh, he sounded so sorry. I'm very angry with him, but he's still my son, you know?" My aunts nodded and said they understood. She said that my grandfather insisted that they pay his bail, which meant Uncle Kenneth would be released soon. I was so thrilled I almost couldn't keep myself from shouting. One aunt asked where would my uncle stay once released.

"Here," my grandmother said.

My aunts were shocked. Did my mom know, they asked?

I knew that answer. There was no way my mom knew her brother, who made her so furious she couldn't even speak his name, would be returning to the place where they grew up together.

My grandmother insisted her sisters keep it quiet, "and you too," she said to me. It was amazing to me how freely my grandmother talked to me about things I should know nothing about, and she hardly knew me.

One aunt asked how Uncle Kenneth looked. I perked up. My grandmother turned to me and said softly, "He looks okay, and he misses you."

One of the aunts cleared her throat and changed the subject quickly as my mom returned.

"So, what school are you going to attend, Jasmine? You know it starts real soon?" one aunt asked.

My mom responded, "She's going to be home-schooled for a little while." The three were shocked.

"Is that a good idea?" my grandmother asked.

My mom briefly explained that it would be the best option since so much had happened.

"*You* were never taught at home," my grandmother said.

"Thank God," my mom mumbled.

"What about your job?" one of the aunts asked.

My mom told them she would be on sabbatical until at least January.

"Oh, I don't know about all that," my grandmother replied, and continued with her argument that not only should I be in a classroom with other children to make friends, my mom and I could tire of each other if we were that close to each other every day. My great aunts agreed. My mom didn't care. In fact, she didn't even argue. She simply stood, grabbed my not-quite-empty plate and my arm, and we left the table with my grandmother and her sisters still talking about the benefits of children attending schools. They didn't seem to have noticed that we had left the table. No one had asked me about I thought.

In the middle of the party, my grandfather called to my grandmother to join him in the living room. An old song was playing on the stereo, and many of my family members were already dancing. Uncle Kenneth and I used to dance together and I had been to Rachel's house for her parent's anniversary party, where everyone had danced. But this was my family I was watching. I wished Uncle Kenneth had been there to see them, too. My grandparents stepped and turned as if they had rehearsed every move. I smiled, watching them have fun. One of my second cousins asked me if I wanted to dance, but I shook my head no. I was just fine watching them. Was this how it had been for Uncle Kenneth growing up?

I started to feel a little angry again when I watched Keisha dance with my grandfather. I didn't have that chance when I was her age. Mrs. Samuels was right about that. Uncle Kenneth took that moment, and so many others, away from me. I envied Keisha. She would always have something I didn't have when I was five.

My grandfather must have known what I was thinking. He danced Keisha over to her father, and then he eased up to me. My grandfather took my hand and said, "C'mon. Make your grand-pop happy and dance with me."

I was nervous at first. I was shaking. I wondered if everyone would stare at us. But then it felt nice. I felt relaxed with him. He turned me around and held my hand. My mom took pictures—she was the only one who was allowed to. I actually started to laugh. When it was over, my grandfather hugged me and then Keisha came up behind me and did the same.

It was late when Keisha sat down next to me on the couch and rested her head on my arm. "You're soft," she said and moved closer. Any closer and she would have been on my lap. The only time she moved was when I stood up to hug family members and say goodbye to them. My grandmother glared from the dining room at a few of them who left with wrapped plates piled high with food, the same ones who kept reaching for food during their entire visit.

That wasn't the only time my grandmother expressed displeasure during the party. She and my great aunts had much to say about the cousins who argued in the backyard over some unpaid debt. And then there were those who asked more than once about TV reporters coming, which made it clear that they only came because they thought they would be interviewed or at least have an appearance on that evening's news.

But mostly, they all treated me like I had been a family member all along. In fact, since I had been in Philadelphia, I had hugged more people than I ever had the whole time I was with Uncle Kenneth. It wasn't easy to do it, either. I had spent so much time alone, and Uncle Kenneth kept me under his watchful eye so much, hugging strangers was not something I had done often. But I didn't feel that I could reject my family's affections, especially little Keisha. She was a sweet and friendly little girl.

After just about all the family had left, I noticed Lucas sitting in a chair. He was around Nathan's age. His mom is my mom's older cousin, and he was an only child. Lucas was dressed in shorts, knee-high socks, and shoes. I noticed he was glaring at me. At first, I tried to ignore him, but he wouldn't take his eyes off me. I would periodically glance back at him. I smiled. He didn't. Then I hoped that one of the times I glanced, he would be looking elsewhere. But he wasn't. It was creepy.

Then Nathan came in. He had something behind his back. I saw trouble. He walked to Lucas, pulled out a water pistol and sprayed him. Lucas shrieked so loud that it made me cringe. Keisha looked over at him strangely. Everyone in the other room ran into the living room to see what had happened.

Then, Keisha blurted out, laughing, "You're all wet, Lucas!"

Aunt Celeste grabbed Nathan and took him away as he cried at being reprimanded once again.

Lucas's mom comforted him. Then I realized that he wasn't weird, just frightened. Maybe he was overprotected like I had been. Still, I knew that if Rachel did something like that to her younger brother, the two of them would have rumbled on the floor.

"Is he all right?" my grandmother called from the other room. "Did he fall?"

Lucas acted like he had. His mom checked him like a doctor looking over someone who had just been wheeled in to an emergency room, and then she said that he was okay. Lucas was still crying when his father came in. He told Lucas to be quiet. Lucas's mother snapped at his father, and they began to argue.

Lucas lowered his head and shook his leg back and forth. He looked embarrassed, but that didn't matter to his parents. They continued battling as Lucas's mom took him upstairs, his father following close behind them.

Uncle Malcolm stood next to my grandfather with his arms crossed, shaking his head. He then said, "They need to stop that. You know that boy will grow up messed up."

My grandfather didn't answer. Instead, he glanced at me.

"You know, he peed himself in school just because his teacher disciplined him," Uncle Malcolm continued.

My grandfather said, "Oh, yeah? That's a shame," in a flat, soft voice, while he kept his eyes on me. He then looked down and slowly walked away.

Lucas's crying fit was the first topic my mom mentioned on the ride home. I thought about Uncle Kenneth while my mom went on about our family. I had to hold in my smile. *He must miss me,* I thought to myself. And he would be out of jail soon. I kept repeating those words over in my mind. I wish there had been more time to hear about my grandparents' visit with him and to ask my grandmother to let Uncle Kenneth know that I couldn't wait to see him. No matter how angry my grandparents were with him, I hoped they were at least trying to forgive him.

"So, do you think you're ready?" my mom asked. *Ready for what?* I thought she was still rambling about the dinner, but she was asking if I was ready to begin therapy. Our first appointment was in a few days. Would it matter if I had said that I wasn't? It was for *me* to recover, wasn't it? The way I saw it, there was no other answer but to tell her that I was. Besides, after Ms. Terri, Ms. Ann, and Mrs. Samuels, I suspected therapy would be more of the same.

Chapter Fifteen

The days leading up to our therapy session were fairly quiet ones. My mom let me call Felicia, but she didn't pick up, so I left a long message. I gave her my mom's phone number, pleading with her to call me. I wished she had answered. I hoped Sabrina was able to talk to her.

I also phoned Rachel. She shouted my name. "Oh my God, what's up? I miss you! Aren't you in Philadelphia? How do you like it?"

I laughed. Just hearing her voice made me so happy. We talked for an hour, until my mom tapped me on the shoulder. I did most of the talking while Rachel listened. She had less to tell me, but talked about how she started babysitting bratty kids, how famous she became because I was the talk of the neighborhood, and about our schoolmates.

My mom finally allowed me to watch television, but she had blocked certain programs. I didn't like that. With Uncle Kenneth, I pretty much watched anything I wanted. I knew some of the shows I watched weren't for kids, like the movies with sex. But I was interested. The most I had ever done with a boy was kiss one on my way home from school. I pulled away from him, nervously, when I felt his penis get hard against my leg. That was my only experience with anything close to sex.

It was still difficult to grasp that my mom had sex at my age, and with someone older. Was it like I had seen in movies? Was it romantic? How did she feel? Was she ashamed because she was so young? Or did she feel special? Uncle Kenneth was always afraid I would get pregnant after I started having my period. That now made sense to me.

Other than my grandmother saying that my mom was quiet like me, I suspected she was very different from me at fourteen. Not just because she had me. I was also sure she wasn't attached to TV the way I had always been. My mom quickly learned that about me. I turned on the TV first thing in the morning. When we came home from somewhere, I grabbed the remote control. After dinner, I sped cleaning up so I could plop in front of the screen. She couldn't have known that the television was my company when living with Uncle Kenneth. Other than him, Rachel and school, I had nothing else.

The night before our first therapy session, I couldn't sleep. At around two in the morning, I quietly went down each step and then turned on the television. As low as the volume was, my mom still came downstairs.

"Why are you watching TV?"

"I couldn't sleep," I said, without even looking at her. The commercial break was over. She came to me, took the remote, and turned off the television.

"Why did you turn it off?" I yelled. It was the first time I'd questioned her authority.

My mom sternly told me to return to bed.

"I said I can't sleep." I didn't realize my tone, until my mom leaned back, put her hands on her hips, and gave me one of those "Who do you think you're talking to young lady?" looks that Uncle Kenneth used to give me.

"You can count to one hundred or sing to yourself. But you are not watching television at this hour."

"What's the big deal? I don't have to get up early." The therapy session was in the afternoon.

"I don't care, Jasmine. Go back to your room."

"But you let me watch TV whenever I want."

"I know, but that's going to stop."

"My dad would let me stay up," I mumbled as I started up the stairs.

"What did you say?"

I didn't mean to go that far, but I was really mad. I couldn't retreat, so I repeated what I had said.

"If you're talking about your Uncle Kenny, let me remind you he's not your father. Kyle Ross is."

That was a sharp blow that hurt me to hear. I lashed out, screaming that my uncle was the only father I had known and he did better than Kyle Ross ever could. Then I asked, "Why do you care so much *now* anyway? You and *Kyle Ross* gave me up. Uncle Kenneth loved me enough to keep me."

I ran up the steps as my mom called to me and shouted that what I had said wasn't true. I slammed my bedroom door. I wanted to pack and leave. I wanted to go live somewhere else—I didn't care where. My mom knocked on the door, but I wouldn't answer. She tried to talk to me through the door. I kept quiet. Then she left me by myself and I was glad. I lay down and cried myself to sleep.

The therapist's office looked like a small living room. My mom and I opened the door to an empty room. We looked at each other. Then she went to the only other door in the room and knocked on it. "Hello," she said and knocked again. We stood, uncertain of what to do.

My mom checked her watch. We were on time. The main door opened. A man in a T-shirt, jeans, and sneakers entered. He had a cardboard cup holder with two cups and a smoothie in his hands. He was breathing hard. He was my therapist, Dr. Vare.

"I'm so sorry I'm late. I was here and then I needed some coffee. So I thought I would bring you an iced tea and a fruit smoothie." He gave my mom and me the drinks. We thanked him.

"You must be Robin and you, Jasmine," he said as he put his hand out to shake ours. Dr. Vare wasn't who I expected at all. He seemed to be the kind of guy who would hang out with Uncle Kenneth, not just because he was black and around my uncle's age, but because he seemed really easy-going. I had thought he would be an older man with a crisp shirt, hard-pressed pants, and reading glasses that he would peer over to look at me after glancing at a folder with all the details of my life. Instead, he was pleasant and didn't seem swayed at all by our surprised expressions. He asked us to have a seat while he went into his office for a moment.

There was one chair against a wall, under a painting of a family in the park. Across from that chair was a round table between two other chairs, and a floor lamp was in the corner. My mom and I sat in the two chairs next to the table. The only sound in the room was the humming from the small white-noise machine near my feet.

We didn't say anything. We hadn't spoken to each other since the night before. I wouldn't admit it, but I didn't like the silence between us. I was starting to like my mom.

Dr. Vare was gone only a few minutes and then asked to see my mom alone first in his office. That was no surprise to me—they always talk to the adults before the kids. I stared at the painting while I sipped the smoothie. The painting reminded me of something that would be in the Sutlers' house.

I wanted to talk to Uncle Kenneth badly. I was jealous of the people in the painting—they looked so happy together. I thought that in time I could be happy with my new family, but I didn't want to be apart from Uncle Kenneth. *Was there a way that I could have both?* But then, where would my real dad fit into all of this? I couldn't say I didn't like him. I just didn't know him. But I really didn't want to get to know him, either. I wanted Uncle Kenneth to be my dad again.

When the door swung open, I was startled. I hadn't realized that I was in such deep thought. My mom was wiping her nose with a tissue when she came out. Dr. Vare held the door open for me, but I couldn't take my eyes off my mom. I felt bad seeing her like that. She managed to smile at me and sat down. There was a part of me that wanted her to come with me into Dr. Vare's office, but then I wanted the chance to tell my side of the story. I wanted someone to really understand how I was feeling, and as I walked into his office, I desperately hoped that Dr. Vare would be listen to me. It would make sense that I would have talked a lot, and that Dr.Vare would have to interrupt me to get a word in, but that didn't happen. I don't know if I was nervous, like a performer who was always ready during rehearsals but scared at show time, or if I had started to doubt that he would actually care about me, but when I sat down on the couch across from him, I shut down. I didn't say much... at first.

"So, how are you doing, Jasmine?" Dr. Vare asked. He seemed sincere.

I answered, "Fine."

"You look fine. In fact, you look very in control for

all that happened to you." He asked if I felt like I was in control or if I felt crazy. When he said "crazy" he shook the top part of his body, with his arms flying, and his head going back and forth. I looked away to keep from giggling. When I thought about it, I certainly didn't feel in control. I was crying myself to sleep every night. After I finally did get to sleep, I would usually wake up in the middle of night, thinking. Sometimes I forgot where I was. Then it would take forever for me to doze back off. I was jittery and tense. Sometimes I couldn't eat because of my nervous stomach. I wasn't in control at all, but I wasn't exactly ready to tell him all of that.

Dr. Vare told me that I could say whatever was on my mind and no one would know. He would keep things confidential. That I didn't have to talk if I didn't want to. Then he stood and went to the window on the right side of me. I didn't reply to everything he told me about what he saw outside, from the birds in the trees to people walking by. He didn't ask any questions. He just let me sit there. Some of his descriptions were funny, but I tightened my stomach to hold in my laughter.

"Oh wow, do you want to see something hilarious?" he asked and began laughing. I didn't move. "You've got to see this, Jasmine." I stayed still for another minute, then slowly stood up and went to the window. I was curious. The one-way street was blocked as a driver struggled to get into a parking space that was clearly too small. The driver bumped the car in back of him over and over, while a line of cars in the middle of the street behind him honked their horns furiously. People walked past and yelled at the driver that he couldn't fit in the space, but that only made him pull out of the space and try again.

Before I knew it, Dr. Vare and I were both laughing

at the other drivers. One woman got out of her car and shouted through the first driver's window to stop trying. He shouted back, showed her his middle finger, and tried to get in the space again.

Someone had called the police, and the first driver started arguing with the officer who came. Then the driver backed up in the space, pulled out, and drove off. The officer wrote down the license plate number, spoke into his radio, and motioned the other drivers to move on. When it was all over, Dr. Vare and I had watched the incident for over fifteen minutes. I had started to feel at ease with him.

I actually enjoyed my therapy sessions. I started meeting with Dr. Vare several days a week. In the first two sessions, he let me talk about anything I wanted. It was like we were simply chatting in his living room. I stayed away from talking about my mom, Uncle Kenneth, my dad, and my new family. Dr. Vare didn't seem to mind. But I should have known that eventually we would begin covering every topic I was trying to avoid. It started when I mistakenly mentioned the movie Uncle Kenneth and I saw where we were photographed. Instead of asking me about the movie, which was what I wanted him to do, Dr. Vare focused on our moving away.

The more questions he asked me, the more silent I became. He even wanted to know what was making me quiet. I shrugged my shoulders and played with a piece of lint that was on the couch.

Dr. Vare leaned towards me. "I know it may be hard for you to believe, Jasmine, but you can trust me," he said.

I wasn't so sure. He reminded me that everything I said in that room would stay there. It had to. It was the law. I didn't think he would tell anyone what I said anyway. I just suspected his goal wasn't to help me, but to make me do what my mom, my dad, and probably even Uncle Kenneth wanted me to do. He kept asking me what was on my mind until I just snapped, "You really want to know?"

"Yes."

"Why?"

"Because what you think and how you feel matters."

"Yeah, right. To who?"

"To me, for one, to your mother, to your father, to your uncle, and to the rest of your family."

I crossed my arms and told Dr. Vare I didn't think he was right. The next session was harder, as he attempted to pull my fears, confusion, and worries out of me. I tested him every chance I had. Dr. Vare never missed a beat. He always challenged me right back.

On the upside, I was finally able to talk freely about Uncle Kenneth and tell Dr. Vare how much I loved and missed him. At first, I had wondered if he would judge me for that, but he didn't. He made me feel like it was okay to think about Uncle Kenneth, which I could only do in his office.

In the third week, my mom joined me during one of the sessions. Dr. Vare told me she would participate in one session a week with me. My mom and I were quiet in the beginning. I thought she was being just as cautious as I was so we wouldn't upset each other. Dr. Vare knew it, too, and he encouraged us to be more open. He asked my mom to say one thing that she was thinking about.

She looked at me and it seemed she pushed herself to say, "I think I'm spoiling Jasmine. I mean, I love her so much, but I think I'm..." My mom's voice faded.

Dr. Vare asked me if I agreed.

Of course I agreed, but what was wrong with that? So what if she wanted to give me everything? I hadn't had her all my life.

"Yes, but Jasmine," my mom said, "you're not listening to me, like when I tell you to turn off the television or to keep your room clean."

Here we go, I thought to myself. Why did she care so much about that?

"My dad didn't," I said.

She tightened her lips and said slowly, "Your Uncle Kenneth is *not* your father."

"He is to me," I said sharply.

Before my mom could speak one word, Dr. Vare cut in. He wanted me to explain what being a father meant.

I replied with a list of what I thought.

Then Dr. Vare asked me to say what made Uncle Kenneth a father to me.

I was confident. I sat up and ran off things I liked about him, but midway I stopped.

Dr. Vare interrupted me and made me think about how life with my uncle really had been. I started to cry. Lying to me hadn't been on my list. Or keeping me from making friends. Or moving me from one place to another. I felt sick inside.

My mom moved closer to me and I cried in her arms.

Dr. Vare wanted my mom to remember that I still loved my uncle. She had to be reminded. I had started to think that my mom was a little happier every time I was upset about Uncle Kenneth. I was glad Dr. Vare said that to her, because it was still so very true that I missed him.

When my mom and I left Dr. Vare's office, we stopped by the supermarket and then headed home. We didn't discuss the session at all, and I didn't ask anything. I loved all the attention she gave me, but at the same time, I didn't want her to think I was some spoiled brat. I still really wanted her to like me. So, I quietly pushed the cart everywhere she instructed me to go. I watched her carefully lift items off shelves, read ingredients, pull out store coupons, compare prices. I felt like we were in there forever, but I didn't complain. I knew she looked at grocery shopping as an opportunity to teach me how to buy the best and save money. Still, I had learned that when shopping with my mom, I had to be extremely patient. Even when I put groceries on the belt, she corrected me to make sure I was arranging them in the right order. Eggs shouldn't be in the same bag as cans. The bread should be by itself so it wouldn't squash. And we wanted to balance everything so the bags wouldn't be too heavy to carry. I didn't have to remember that much for a math test. But it turned out to be a good evening—until later, when I heard my mom scream "You can't be serious!" from her bedroom.

I was in the dining room, setting the table for dinner when I heard her yell louder than I ever had. She was furious, and there could have been only one reason why. My suspicions were confirmed when I heard my mom ask my grandmother how my grandparents could do it.

I knew what "it" was. They had not only paid bail for Uncle Kenneth, but he would definitely stay at my grandparent's house until his trial began.

My mom slammed the door to her bedroom. It didn't matter. She was so loud on the phone that I could still hear her as I sat at the bottom of the stairs. If I had had no clue how angry my mom was with Uncle Kenneth, I certainly knew then. She was unforgiving, and her accusations were strong against him. She felt betrayed by my grandparents, who apparently had put up their house as collateral to pay the bail. I understood that feeling. Although Uncle Kenneth had betrayed both of us, I still longed to see him.

I silently climbed the stairs as I listened intently to my mom. She began weeping, telling my grandmother that she didn't understand how hard it had been. My grandmother must have described how she had felt because my mom responded, "For *you? You* never had to give up me or Celeste or Kenny!"

My grandmother then said something that really made my mom explode.

"Yes, I know what I did, Mom! You don't have to remind me! And I know what Dad had to do because of it! It's was my fault that your plans for Kyle and Celeste didn't work out the way you wanted and that I shamed the family, but I needed you!"

It was quiet and then my mom said, "If you were really sorry, you wouldn't help Kenny." She pleaded with my grandmother to reconsider letting Uncle Kenneth stay there. Whatever my grandmother said, it made my mom abruptly end the call.

I remembered at the family dinner that my grandmother said it was my grandfather who insisted Uncle Kenneth come back to live with them. I knew at that dinner my mom wouldn't be happy with his decision. I just couldn't have imagined how unhappy she would be.

My mom phoned Mr. Shane—the man I had thought was her boyfriend. She was crying like a child. He offered to come to our house, but she insisted she would be fine and then she started crying all over again. It was the first time I'd heard my mom in so much pain. Until then, she had been strong. Even when she simply said "no comment" to reporters, she did it with style. She always tried to comfort me, but on the phone in her bedroom she sounded wounded, with different emotions all mixed together.

She sounded like me.

I began to really understand my mom's feelings about what had happened. I had thought so much about myself. I hadn't realized what she was going through, especially feeling that she had embarrassed the whole family when she was fourteen.

But now I had questions—what did she mean about my grandmother's plans for my dad and Aunt Celeste, and what did my grandfather have to do? My mom had carried more on her shoulders than I knew. I struggled between staying where I was at the top of the stairs until my mom came out of her room, or going in to her room to console her. She had been silent for a few minutes after she hung up with Mr. Shane. Maybe he calmed her, but I opted to knock on her door anyway. I still had not called my mom by her name, or Mom, or Mommy.

She opened the door with a forced smile. It was a miserable attempt. I asked her if she was all right, a dumb question. She said she was okay, an unconvincing answer. She asked me if I needed anything. I shook my head no. I asked her why she had been crying. She waved her hand and shook her head. She said she needed a few minutes and would come downstairs. She closed the door and I went back downstairs to wait. I didn't even turn on the TV.

I saw myself in the way my mom pretended there wasn't a problem when she finally came downstairs. That's what I had been doing since this all began. Her face was a little clearer. She chatted like she hadn't just called her brother every cruel name you could call someone or hadn't cried hysterically because of him.

Watching her convinced me that I didn't want to be a performer anymore. I remembered when Dr. Vare said in one of the sessions that I should get in the habit of expressing myself to my mom, so I did. I confessed.

After all the times I'd eavesdropped, I told her that I had just listened to her conversations. My mom looked at me, surprised. I wasn't exactly sure why. I mean, we didn't live in a mansion, where her bedroom was in an entirely different wing of the house.

"How much did you hear?"

"Everything," I said. Then I frantically apologized because she exhaled deeply. She rubbed her face. I kept saying I was sorry.

"It's okay, Jasmine, really," she said. She thought for a minute, took my hand and rubbed hers over mine. She stared at our hands. "You really want to see your uncle, don't you?"

I told her I did.

"Well, you know where he'll be in a few days, so I'll take you to him."

Chapter Sixteen

The visit with my Uncle Kenneth was approved. This time, there wouldn't be any reporters waiting for me. My story had been replaced by celebrity gossip, crime stories, and government scandals.

My mom drove slower than she usually did as we went to my grandparents' house, which didn't bother me. I knew she wasn't exactly thrilled about seeing her brother. I kept reminding myself, she was going to see him for the first time since she was fifteen. I wondered if she was nervous. I sure was. But then I thought my mom was probably way too angry to be anxious.

My grandparents' block was quiet, like my mom had said it usually was. We parked right in front of the house. My mom turned off the car but didn't move.

"Do you want me to go in by myself?" I asked.

She shook her head no. She pulled down the sun visor and looked at herself in the vanity mirror. She closed it up and we got out of the car and went to my grandparents' front door.

As soon as my grandmother opened the door, I saw Uncle Kenneth jump up from the couch. My mom acted emotionless. She barely looked at my grandmother.

Before I could really get a good look at him, Uncle Kenneth came over and hugged me tight. It was like we were the only ones in the room. I didn't think about my mom, my grandparents, or Aunt Celeste and Uncle

Malcolm. All I could focus on was the warmth of my uncle holding me.

"Okay, you two, let go of each other," my grandfather said.

Uncle Kenneth wiped his eyes. I took a good look at him. He had lost weight. He looked like he had aged a few years.

We sat down on the couch, my grandmother was on the other side of Uncle Kenneth. Everyone else sat in chairs around the living room.

Uncle Kenneth asked me how I was. I told him I was doing well.

"I just know you are. Your mom is taking great care of you."

I turned to look at her. I had never seen such rage in anyone's face as I saw in hers. She glared at Uncle Kenneth and, when he looked at her, she looked away from him.

"You look beautiful, Robin," Uncle Kenneth said.

She ignored him.

"Robin, didn't you hear your brother?" my grandmother asked.

My mom ignored her, too. Uncle Kenneth looked back at me and said I had gained some weight.

"Yeah, well, you lost some weight," I said jokingly.

We kept talking like there was no one with us, but I could feel my mom's anger from across the room—and not only hers. Aunt Celeste was staring at Uncle Kenneth just as hard. As wonderful as the reunion with Uncle Kenneth was for me, it was also becoming very uncomfortable. It was clear that my mom and Aunt Celeste were struggling very hard to get through how joyous Uncle Kenneth, my grandparents, and I all were. It eventually became too much. My mom stood up and said, "I can't take this.

C'mon, Jasmine, we're going." The room became quiet. I frowned at her. I had no intention of leaving.

"You just got here," my grandmother said.

"Yeah, and now we're leaving. C'mon, Jasmine." I didn't get up.

"Please don't be like this," Uncle Kenneth said to her.

"Like what?" my mom yelled. "What? You don't want *me* to take Jasmine away from *you*, like *you* took her away from *me?*"

Uncle Kenneth stood up and went to my mom. He touched her arm.

She jerked away from him and said sternly, "Don't you dare touch me."

Uncle Kenneth raised his hands and backed off. He said sadly, "I'm so sorry for keeping you from your daughter, Robin." His voice cracked. "Please know that I love you and..."

My mom slapped his face and screamed at him, "You *are* sorry! You're nothing but a *sorry* asshole!"

My grandparents ran over. I jumped up and ran to Uncle Kenneth. Before my mom could hit Uncle Kenneth again, my grandfather grabbed her. Uncle Kenneth brushed away my grandmother, who was trying to nurse him. Aunt Celeste and Uncle Malcolm had stood up as well.

I was frightened. I hadn't known my mom that long, but I was sure she wasn't a violent person. She did say at the hotel that she would have kicked Uncle Kenneth's ass if he had been there. I didn't think she actually meant it.

"I'm okay," Uncle Kenneth said and fell back on the couch. He threw his head back and rubbed the side of his face.

My grandfather let go of my mom and roared, "That's

enough!" His voice boomed and it shook me. The room became quiet again.

I was very scared. It seemed like I had just met my family, and already they—we—were falling apart.

No one spoke for a few minutes. My mom sat back in her chair and covered her face. My grandmother asked if I should go upstairs.

"No, this is a family meeting, and she's family," my mom snapped.

I was glad. I didn't want to go anywhere.

Aunt Celeste broke the silence. "Why did you do it?" she asked Uncle Kenneth.

"You know why I did it. It was for Robin and Kyle." He looked so sad.

"No, that's what we thought at the time. Why did you really offer to take Jasmine?"

Uncle Kenneth said he didn't know what Aunt Celeste was talking about.

"We were kids, Kenny. You were the adult, but you were only twenty-one. Why would you, when you were that young, want to take care of a baby that wasn't even yours?" Aunt Celeste was calm.

Uncle Kenneth was getting fidgety.

"I made a sacrifice for Robin and Kyle."

Uncle Malcolm said, "You know, sacrifices in families are very common."

Aunt Celeste shook her head at him as if to say, "Not now," and that was the last we heard from Uncle Malcolm.

Then Aunt Celeste turned to Uncle Kenneth and told him that if he really had been concerned about my mom and dad, and only wanted to make a sacrifice, he would have brought me back as originally planned.

Uncle Kenneth shook his head. His jaw tightened. "What do you want me to say, Celeste?"

"The truth, damn it," my mom blurted.

Uncle Kenneth yelled that he *was* speaking the truth. He asked everyone to remember how crazy it had been when I was born and how scared my mom was. He reminded them that, at the time, everyone was angry at each other and his idea brought my mom and dad some peace—they could go to school and know that I was okay.

Everyone sat strangely still.

"All right," Uncle Kenneth said after a few seconds, "I kept Jasmine and I shouldn't have. And I apologize for the hurt I've caused. But I couldn't let her go. I loved her. I was raising her. I mean, look at her." He opened his hand in my direction. "She was as beautiful as a baby as she is now. She needed me. I held her. I fed her. I changed her. I took good care of her. We were as close as any father and daughter." Uncle Kenneth's voice quavered. His eyes were wet with tears.

He told my mom and Aunt Celeste, "You two act like I had a plan within a plan, like it was my intention to keep Jasmine all along."

No one spoke. My mom and Aunt Celeste looked at Uncle Kenneth intensely.

"Don't look at me like that. Do you *really* think that's how it was? I swear I was going to return her. I just loved her so much. *She felt like my own daughter.*"

"But she was *mine!* I named her Alexis and she was mine!" my mom shrieked. My grandfather returned to her and put his arm around her. She pulled away from him. She asked my grandparents how they could let Uncle Kenneth live there after what he did.

My stomach turned. This wasn't a television episode. This was real. These people cried and screamed because of me. They cried for me as a baby. They missed me. My uncle had me and lost me. My mom lost me and got me back. And because of me, they were tearing themselves apart and away from each other.

"He's our son!" my grandmother shouted.

"And I'm your daughter!" my mom shouted back. "Tell me something. Did it ever occur to you that we still wouldn't know where they were if it hadn't been for Jasmine's friend calling the police?"

My grandparents looked at Uncle Kenneth for an answer. I knew that my mom was right. There was no telling where he and I would be if it wasn't for Felicia. I may have never known any of my family, not even that I had one. I realized that Felicia *had* done the right thing. I wouldn't doubt that ever again.

"You don't know that, Robin," Uncle Kenneth responded angrily.

"Oh, I do. You may not want to admit it even to yourself, but you two would still be somewhere out there, and we would still be here wondering where you were," my mom said.

The room was still again. After a few minutes, my mom decided it was time leave. Uncle Kenneth asked if he could speak to me alone first.

"You've got to be kidding," my mom snapped.

"Oh, for goodness sake, Robin," my grandmother blurted, "What's the problem? It's not like Kenny's going to take her again."

"Oh God, Doreen," my grandfather said.

Uncle Kenneth hung his head. "No, I wouldn't do that."

"Wouldn't you?" my mom yelled.

Uncle Kenneth looked at her directly. "No, Robin, I wouldn't."

My mom didn't trust him. She refused to let us be by ourselves. Uncle Kenneth didn't want to make me uneasy, so he asked that everyone leave the living room except my mom.

"I heard that things didn't go well with meeting your father," he said.

My expression changed. Why did my uncle have to bring that up?

"Jasmine, you've got to be nice to him."

"Why?"

"Because he's... your father."

I sat back against the couch and crossed my arms. Now *I* was angry. I asked Uncle Kenneth if we could talk about it another time.

He told me that my dad had visited him in jail. My dad hadn't held back on what he thought of Uncle Kenneth. "He let me have it and I deserved it, Jasmine."

"You sure did," my mom charged.

Uncle Kenneth ignored her.

"I don't know if I'll like him," I blurted without thinking. I was a little embarrassed to say that in front of my mom. I knew how important it was to her that I develop a relationship with my dad.

Uncle Kenneth pleaded with me to give him a chance.

"He wants to take *your* place," I said. Tears stung my eyes.

"No, Jasmine. All those years I was trying to take *his*."

Uncle Kenneth insisted my dad was a good man. He

Lisa R. Nelson

said we would have a lot in common, if I only let myself find out. He asked me to promise him that I would try to get to know him.

"But what about you?" Now I *was* crying. I just wanted Uncle Kenneth to be my dad again.

"I'm not going anywhere. Even if I'm sentenced to jail, I'll always, always be your uncle. Not your dad, Jasmine. Your uncle." He hugged me and kissed me on the top of my head.

"Can I ask you something?" By then, I had forgotten that my mom was in the room.

"Anything."

"Why did you tell me you had a brother?"

Uncle Kenneth smiled and replied that there was a time when he wanted a brother, so he told me that so I wouldn't be able to learn who I really was.

I asked him who was the woman in the picture he had said was my mom. He admitted it was a photograph of an old girlfriend.

"Wow," my mom suddenly snapped and shook her head.

Everyone came back into the room—they had had second thoughts about the three of us being in a room without them.

"Don't worry, I won't touch your precious son," my mom said sarcastically to my grandparents.

"That's not necessary," my grandfather said.

"Do you blame her?" Aunt Celeste asked.

My grandfather didn't answer her. But my family's battle had begun again. I couldn't have known that the argument would be so intense that no one held back from revealing the full truth, even in front of me.

Chapter Seventeen

It wasn't supposed to be Robin and Kyle. They weren't supposed to meet each other when he visited the house. After all, my grandfather had spent time trying to figure how Kyle and Celeste could meet. My paternal grandfather was my maternal grandfather's boss, and they thought my dad and my aunt, both high school seniors, would be a good match. They joked about it at first, but the more they talked, the more it made sense. My dad was smart and had had girlfriends before, but the relationships didn't last long. Aunt Celeste, her parents thought, needed someone who was a little more polished than the boys she brought home. So my grandfathers decided they would introduce my dad and Aunt Celeste at the annual company picnic, where employees could bring their families. It had been a nice Saturday afternoon in September. Uncle Kenneth didn't go. At his age, he thought he would have a much better time with his friends. My grandmothers arranged for my dad and Aunt Celeste to sit together. They included them in discussions and said things like, "Kyle, doesn't Celeste look nice?" and "Celeste, isn't Kyle smart?"

They asked my dad to escort Aunt Celeste to the family car because my grandmother "forgot" something. Meanwhile, my mom couldn't keep her eyes off my dad. He caught her looks and smiled every time. He liked her attention. She liked his smile. Aunt Celeste wasn't that impressed with him. My dad wasn't taken with Aunt Celeste. When my dad later visited the house, Aunt Celeste began to notice how often and how long my mom would remain in the room with them. In time, the three of them conspired so my dad and my mom could be together.

It was cute at first. My mom would fix her hair and carefully choose her outfits on my dad's visiting days. Aunt Celeste felt a thrill in fooling her parents, especially when my grandparents went out. They left Aunt Celeste in charge, and she and my mom would have company— my dad and whoever Aunt Celeste wanted to see. Uncle Kenneth didn't particularly like my mom and dad secretly dating, but Aunt Celeste convinced him it was just a simple crush, nothing serious. But then my mom began talking differently. She not only spoke about my dad constantly, she was using the word *love* to describe her feelings. Even Aunt Celeste became worried. She tried to bring my mom back down to earth, but it was too late. My dad wasn't as attracted to my mom as she was to him, but they were close enough to spend more time sneaking in my mom's bedroom than even Aunt Celeste knew.

Aunt Celeste was the first to find out my mom was pregnant. They were both scared, but decided together that my mom should wait before telling anyone, even my dad. The news didn't sit well. There was plenty of blame. My mom was a fast girl, according to my dad's parents. My dad took advantage of a young girl, according to my mom's parents. My mom and Aunt Celeste must not have had any discipline for the pregnancy to happen in my mom's own bedroom, according to my dad's parents. My dad should have been shown more control since he was older, according to my mom's parents.

Then the questions arose. Would my mom's pregnancy ruin my dad's plans for college? How could my mom go to school while she raised a child? How would my parents be able to afford me? They were too young for the responsibility, weren't they? After long discussions, my grandparents on both sides made decisions. My dad would attend his chosen university, as planned. My mom would complete high school. Cousins—a newly married couple who wanted a baby—would take me in temporarily. They didn't live far away, so my mom could visit anytime she wanted, as long as it didn't interfere with her schoolwork.

My mom begged to keep me. She was sorry that my grandfather had to quit his job, where he had a promising future, because it was extremely difficult for him to continue working under my dad's father. She apologized every day for embarrassing the family. My mom was sad for days, weeks, months. Aunt Celeste tried to help my mom feel better, but nothing cheered her up as much as Uncle Kenneth's suggestion. He could take care of everything. What did he have to give up? Since he had recently graduated from college, he was working at a job he didn't particularly like. He didn't have a girlfriend to break up with. And he would only keep me for a couple of years, and bring me back when my parents were older. At first, my parents thought the idea wouldn't work. Uncle Kenneth persuaded them. He had thoroughly thought out the plan. Uncle Kenneth bought a car—without my grandparents knowing—with the money he had saved for his own apartment. A month after I was born and a few days before my mom was to give me up to her cousins, she and my dad handed me over to Uncle Kenneth. The cousins who were supposed to take me were devastated, but they eventually had their own child—Lucas.

Chapter Eighteen

Dr. Vare didn't have to ask me how I felt about my family's latest revelations. I was ready to do most of the talking. I felt that I was to real blame for so much of the mess. After all, the lies and secrets began when I was born.

"Think about it," I said to Dr. Vare. "I'm the center of my family's discord."

"How do you know that?' he asked me.

"Aren't you the professional?" I asked. "You mean you can't see it?"

"I guess I should have taken a few more college classes. Explain it to me?"

I didn't care for his sarcasm, but I explained anyway. Actually, I just repeated myself. I didn't really say anything new. But Dr. Vare listened and suggested something that I hadn't considered.

"Start asking your family what it was like for them before and then when you were born."

I felt like I was talking to an idiot. Didn't he understand that everyone was angry?

"No, Jasmine, don't ask how they felt when you were taken by your uncle or how scared your fourteen-year-old mother was when she found out she was pregnant. Ask your family how they felt about you. Only you."

I didn't have a chance to ask my mom on the car ride home. She was talking the details of my home schooling, the materials she still had to buy, and my daily schedule.

"We have to get you a library card."

That was the only thing my mom said directly to me. So I thought I would ask her when we returned home. No such luck. Mr. Shane called. I knew that was going to be a long conversation. While she talked, I took clothes out of the dryer. Since seeing Dr. Vare, my mom started to give me chores. *She* could be sloppy, but she had a "do-as-I-say, not-as-I-do" attitude.

It wasn't like I didn't have any chores with Uncle Kenneth. I swept and mopped the floors. I washed dishes and I did laundry with him. I just never had a *mom* tell me to do those things. At first, I didn't like it. But then, it was okay.

When I noticed that one of my shirts wasn't in the dryer, I went to her. She was still on the phone. She put up her finger to tell me to wait. Then she gave me the phone. I wondered what Mr. Shane wanted and then the voice on the other end said, "What's up Jaaassssmiine?"

I screamed when I heard Felicia's voice. I was so excited. My mom smiled. Apparently, she was talking with Mr. Shane, when the other call came in. She spoke to Felicia to thank her for helping to bring me home.

"Your mom sounds really nice," Felicia said, and she didn't sound sad either.

"She is." I shifted the subject away from my mom. I didn't want to risk upsetting Felicia when I hadn't spoken to her in so long. I flooded her with so many questions that she had to cut me off just so she could answer them.

"The hotel is gone." It was the first thing Felicia told me. She said she went by it every day to watch its transformation.

"My father sold it to a company that's turning it into a bowling alley."

I was shocked that Felicia was so calm. She *had* to miss the hotel if she visited the building every day, but she wasn't agitated at all. I didn't have to comfort her, tell her it was going to be okay, or try to cheer her up. She even sounded happy that her dad got a large amount of money for the hotel, which he told her would be used for her college tuition.

"Your what?" I asked excitedly.

"You heard me, *college*. I'm starting in January." Right after Felicia, her dad, and Sabrina left me at the police station, her dad finalized the deal. "I was depressed, which was why I couldn't call you back."

Although I didn't say it, I knew the hotel sale wasn't the only reason Felicia wasn't able to talk to me. I could have asked if she was sad after she heard me say that my mom was alive, but I kept it to myself. She didn't seem upset about it anymore. Maybe Sabrina spoke to her. But Felicia was comfortable enough to return to the subject of my mom. I gave her an earful about my parents, the first meeting with my dad, my family, and therapy.

"Wow, girl. I thought a lot had been going on with me. It's been nothing compared to you."

I agreed, but it seemed to be more than that. I felt a little older as I talked with Felicia. I felt closer to her age than I did before. *She* even said I sounded different.

"Not so whiney," she said.

I laughed. She may have been right. It wasn't that I was *trying* to be mature. But it made sense that, after all I had been through, I had grown up some.

I asked Felicia about Sabrina.

"I'm not sure what she's really thinking, but she's

slowing down. She's seeing her clients less and less, and she dropped some of them all together."

What was she going to do, get a real job? Felicia didn't know, but she said that Sabrina had saved plenty of money and had an apartment in the same building with Felicia and her dad.

"Does she still watch over you like a hawk?"

"More than ever, especially since she's working less. But it's okay. We're managing."

It sounded like they were all managing pretty well. Felicia didn't mention Ricky once. She told me that when I got a cell phone she would send me some pictures. I didn't know when that would be. As I was becoming settled in my new environment, my mom was still being overly cautious.

"It's going to take some time. She lost you once. She just doesn't want to lose you again." Then Felicia stressed that I should try to understand my mom's view. Funny thing was, I was already following that advice. But I didn't have time to tell Felicia more about that, because my mom told me it was time to get off the phone. Before we hung up, Felicia quickly said, "It's good that you found your family, especially your mom. Relish all the time you have with her." We then said our goodbyes. I was already excited about the next time I would hear Felicia on the other end of the phone.

Chapter Nineteen

He was stumped. My dad wasn't sure what to say. He called one afternoon while my mom was outside. He asked me to let her know he called. I thought about the promise I made to Uncle Kenneth. I forced myself to tell him that I had started reading the book he gave me, which was true.

"That's great, Jasmine. Do you like it? I mean, is it interesting?"

It was. Actually, it was the nicest book about animals I'd ever seen. I didn't go that far. I just said him, "Yes, it's really good."

"Good. Good."

It was obvious he didn't know what to say next. I wasn't exactly sure either. So, after an uncomfortable moment of silence, my dad said, "Well, tell your mother that I called."

I blurted out, "Can I ask you something?"

"Of course."

I asked my dad if he was happy or upset when I was born. He paused, and I felt my heart pounding.

"I was upset that I wasn't prepared to take care of you, but I was thrilled when you were born. I still am."

I didn't know how to respond to that. Was he just saying it so I would like him? Maybe he *was* telling the truth. According to Uncle Kenneth, my dad let him have it because he was so angry with him. And my dad did spend money to try to find me when he found a job after college.

"Hello? Are you still there, Jasmine?"

"Uh-huh. I'm here. I have to go now."

"Okay. It was nice talking to you."

I got off the phone real fast. Why was he being so nice to me even after I ran from him when we first met? He never pushed me after that. He frequently called my mom to ask about me, but didn't ask to talk to me. He waited for me to reach out to him. Perhaps Uncle Kenneth was right, and I should give my dad a chance. But I didn't want to give him the wrong idea—I didn't want him to start bossing me around. I would have to be careful with my dad. Since he was waiting for *me, I* would take my time. I would have to. I was still too nervous to do anything else.

Chapter Twenty

I was excited. It was mid-October and my grandparents had prepared Sunday dinner for my birthday—my real birthday. I was going to be fifteen years old. My mom and I had a long conversation, because she said it would be too difficult for her to be there with Uncle Kenneth. She was also afraid that she would ruin the dinner, and she didn't want to interfere with the celebration. I understood. She couldn't trust that she could keep her mouth shut. She was still terribly upset, although she tried to hide it. I was learning about her. She wasn't as good an actor as Uncle Kenneth or me.

Surprisingly, it wasn't stressful at home. Together, my mom and I, with Dr. Vare's help, were figuring out how to be mother and daughter. We were even learning to get through talks that made us uncomfortable. Like the time she asked me if I wanted to keep Jasmine as my name. I didn't know. It may seem strange, but I hadn't thought about it.

"You could be Jasmine Alexis. Or Alexis Jasmine."

"What about Jasixis?" I asked jokingly.

"Or Alexmine?" my mom asked, laughing.

We then went back and forth trying to outdo each other with crazy combinations of the two names.

I'm used to Jasmine, but I do like Alexis. And I know it would have made my mom happy if I wanted to be called Alexis.

I found out that my mom could be quirky. She didn't realize it, but she was more like her mother than she realized. But she could also be very serious, like when she was on the phone, choosing a doctor for me. She asked questions like she worked for the C.I.A.

She was extra careful with my home schooling. She was online all the time researching materials, figuring out how to schedule our days, and she studied everything she could to make sure she could check my homework questions. It was weird at first. I was used to being in a classroom, but the lessons turned out to be okay. After all, my mom *is* a teacher.

I wished she would have wanted to go to my grandparents' house for my birthday. I would have loved to tell my grandmother in front of my mom how it had been a good idea for me to learn at home.

But my mom wasn't having it. She had planned something special for me but it was a surprise. So Aunt Celeste and Uncle Malcolm picked me up, and I rode in the back seat with Keisha and Nathan. The whole ride was filled with Keisha yelling, "Stop, Nathan! Leave me alone, Nathan!" after which Aunt Celeste and Uncle Malcolm would scream the same thing. He never listened to them before, so I couldn't figure out why they thought he would decide to listen to them now. He stuck out his tongue at me. He dug his finger far up his nose and attempted to spread that same finger on my arm before I pushed him away as forcefully as I could. Then he returned to bugging his sister, while I swore to myself I would turn down any invitation to anywhere that involved a ride with Nathan in the car.

My grandparents didn't have to ask me why my mom wasn't with me. She hadn't visited their house since the family argument. They and Uncle Kenneth greeted me with hugs and kisses. It was ironic—for so long I couldn't mention Uncle Kenneth's name, and at the dinner no one mentioned my mom's name.

I supposed Aunt Celeste give my mom a full report of who said what, about what, and when. My mom could have simply asked me, but Dr. Vare had suggested she try not to put me in the middle of my family's dispute.

Dinner was tasty. Everyone sang "Happy Birthday," and I received lots of gifts. It was like a birthday dinner on a TV show. I helped prepare the table and then helped to clean up afterward. When the dishes were done, my grandmother asked me to get her glasses off her dresser in her bedroom. She was very specific and also very wrong about where they were. I had to look around, and then I noticed it. In the middle of different creams and oils, my name was on one of the bottles. No one mentioned it, but they had to know. Of all the names to choose, Uncle Kenneth had picked Jasmine. I grabbed the bottle and my grandmother's glasses, and ran downstairs. I pulled Uncle Kenneth away from everyone.

"Is this why you named me Jasmine?" I asked as I showed him the bottle of Jasmine oil. He smiled. It was.

"Where did you get this?" he asked.

I told him where.

"She still uses it," Uncle Kenneth said.

My grandmother would pour some of the oil in her bath when Uncle Kenneth was growing up. It wasn't the only oil she used, but it was the one Uncle Kenneth liked.

"You remind me of this," he said and looked at the bottle. "Jasmine has a sweet scent. I remembered how nice the bathroom smelled after your grandmother was done. It didn't take me long to decide to name you Jasmine."

I didn't know how to feel about that—but my mom was right. I wasn't *his* daughter. Maybe she had a special reason why she picked Alexis. There could have been a story behind that name—I would have to ask her. Maybe I should accept her choice and put Alexis before Jasmine. But then it hit me. I didn't have to make the decision by myself. I had a mom *and* a dad, although I had trouble talking to him. I had grandparents on both sides, even though I hadn't yet met my dad's side of the family. I had Felicia. I even had a therapist I could talk to. I was sure that with all the people around me, I would have a name I could be happy with, a name that was right for me.

I went outside on my grandparents' back porch. It was a cool, sunny day. Keisha came out to sit next to me, followed by Nathan. He began teasing her again. I stood up and waved him over to me. I whispered, "You know what we can do to really get Keisha?" His eyes got big. I told him to follow me. That wasn't a problem. When we reached my grandfather's flimsy hedges, Nathan asked, "So what are we going to do?" I turned to him and said, "We're not going to do anything. You're going to leave your sister and me alone." I picked him up, while he flailed his arms, and threw him on top of the hedge. As he wiggled, he sunk into the twigs and bushes. When I reached the steps, Keisha was laughing. Nathan made his way out of the hedge, crying. By then Aunt Celeste and my grandfather had come out of the house. Keisha pointed at her brother and said, "You look like a reindeer." He did, with the way the twigs were arranged on top of his head.

"How did this happen?" Aunt Celeste asked Nathan, as she wiped his face.

I looked sharply at him. He looked at me.

"I, uh, I was playing and fell in," he whined.

Aunt Celeste grabbed his arm, pulling him inside and reprimanding him. Keisha had had her moment and followed them inside.

I returned to the steps. My grandfather grunted as he sat down beside me. We chatted for a few minutes about the weather and his hope that his collards and tomatoes would grow well.

I hadn't planned to say it, but "I wish my mom was here" popped out of my mouth.

He said he, too, wished she were there. For some reason, he was sure we would all have dinner again, even with my mom. I wasn't so certain.

"She'll come around. She just needs a little time."

More than a little, I told him.

"You know, your uncle called me." I wasn't sure what my grandfather was talking about. I looked at him, puzzled. He stared straight ahead.

"He called me two days after he left with you."

No one knew that Uncle Kenneth kept calling and hanging up the phone on my grandmother until my grandfather finally answered. Uncle Kenneth was panicked. He didn't think he could handle me.

"I could hear you screaming in the background. He said you wouldn't stop crying. He told me he rocked you, fed you, and changed you. Nothing worked."

My grandfather had to calm down Uncle Kenneth before he could tell him how to calm me down. He suggested that Uncle Kenneth rub and lightly pat my back. I burped and stopped crying. Uncle Kenneth was relieved. My grandfather saw it as an opportunity.

"I said everything I could possibly think of to get your uncle to come back home." And a couple of times during the conversation, my grandfather thought he was actually close to persuading Uncle Kenneth to not only tell him where we were, but to allow my grandfather to come and get us. Uncle Kenneth called a few more times, whenever he was frightened, but he never left a phone number or an address. He didn't know what he really had done by agreeing to be take me. My inability to communicate other than through cries and facial expressions made it tough for Uncle Kenneth.

"Then I didn't hear from him. Every time the phone rang I answered it, for two weeks straight. Your grandmother started to worry if *I* was okay." My grandfather was concerned. He thought it was a good thing that Uncle Kenneth had kept calling. He really thought he could get through to him. But after those few calls, he didn't hear from him again.

"Nobody knows about this," my grandfather said solemnly. He didn't ask, but I had the feeling he knew I wouldn't say a word about it. "Leaving you with Lucas's parents wouldn't have been a good idea.Don't get me wrong, they're nice people, but we shouldn't have made Robin agree to that." He paused and looked at me.

"I'm glad you're here."

"You are?" I asked.

"Sure."

"But since I've been here, everything has fallen apart. Mom is upset. She doesn't talk to you and..." I hesitated. He waited. "And Grand-mom."

There, I'd said it. I'd called them Mom and Grand-mom. It wasn't as difficult as I thought it would be. And just like that, I decided I would call my grandparents Grand-mom and Grand-pop.

My grandfather cut me off to tell me that *I* was

holding the family together. I couldn't figure that one out. He said the last time everyone was in one room together was before Uncle Kenneth took me away.

"Now, yes, there's a lot of yelling, but that has nothing to do with *you*. Your uncle was the one that was wrong. You, you're an angel. Don't forget that." My grandfather patted the top of my head and went inside.

I looked around the backyard again. I had really enjoyed myself at dinner, but I knew that Uncle Kenneth's future would soon be decided in court. I was nervous every time I thought about it. And he wasn't himself. I caught him smoking a cigarette, which he quit years ago. He still hadn't gained his weight back. He hardly went out. Aunt Celeste told me that he had been spit on, cursed at, and called all kinds of names. My uncle was different than he had been when he was my dad. He was always happy to see me, but even then, I could tell he was pushing himself to behave normally. Other days, he just wanted to talk about our life together.

I didn't want to testify against him. My mom and Dr. Vare reminded me that telling the truth didn't mean I was going against Uncle Kenneth. Because I was only fifteen, I would be talking to just the judge in front of a camera, and my testimony would be shown during the trial without me having to get on the stand before the jury. Because I was considered a witness, I wasn't allowed to attend the trial, and I don't think my mom would have allowed me to. I wished I could be there for Uncle Kenneth, but it would have meant fighting with my mom, and I was just so tired of fighting.

I was still struggling with relationship with Uncle Kenneth. I slipped up sometimes and called to him my dad. I even kept calling him for advice when my mom urged me to get in the habit of asking my real dad for his opinion. Sometimes Uncle Kenneth wasn't available for me, and I wondered if he was avoiding me. I didn't call my dad. I talked to him when he called our house. It was hard to rely on him like I had with Uncle Kenneth. The longest phone conversation I had with him lasted less than fifteen minutes. He asked if he could visit me to give me a birthday gift. How could I say no? I was still uneasy about seeing him. I asked my mom if she would stay in the room with us. She said she would. But things were changing. Although there was so much discord in my family, for the first time I didn't feel alone. I felt I could talk to any one of them. It was starting to sink in that they really loved me. I had choices.

I had choices, right there on my grandparent's back steps. I could stay there. I could go in the house. I could play with Keisha. I could watch the football game on TV with my grandfather, Uncle Kenneth, and Uncle Malcolm. I could help Aunt Celeste or my grandmother. Or I could even make a phone call to Felicia or Rachel. I smiled at the thought that I had options.

Just then, Keisha came outside and sat next to me.

"Whatchu doin' out here?"

"Thinking."

"All by yourself?"

I nodded.

"That's boring."

I laughed. I asked her how Nathan was.

"He's crying again." She smiled at me. "Did you like your birthday?"

I told her I did and that I loved her gift. She had made a card and a beaded bracelet from a jewelry-making kit.

"I like you, Jasmine."

"I like you, too."

"I always wanted a big sister."

Lisa R. Nelson

I thought "always" was a little much for a five year old, but it was cute.

"You know what's funny, Keisha? I've always wanted one, too."

"That *is* funny." She giggled. "Tell Aunt Robin she missed a lot of fun."

"I will."

"Jasmine?"

"Yes?"

"Can you keep a secret?"

I grinned. I thought about Mrs. Warner's phone number and sneaking to see Felicia. I thought about it all. I smiled at Keisha.

"Well, can you?"

"Keisha, honey," I answered as I put my arm around her. "You have no idea how well I can keep a secret. No idea at all."

Acknowledgments

This novel couldn't have been written without my instructor, publisher, and friend, Victoria A. Brownworth, to whom I am enormously grateful. I truly value her guidance and expertise, and am thankful for her continuing belief in my work. Thank you to my writing circle of friends, Joanne Dahme, Jane Shaw, and Diane DeKelb-Rittenhouse, for sweetly welcoming me into the fold—our weekly meetings go well beyond literature. Kudos to Judith Redding for her remarkable talents as a copy editor. Special appreciation to my sisters Rachelle Nelson and Nadine Nelson-Smith and my nephew Christopher A. Nelson for their ongoing encouragement and faith. Words cannot express my sincere gratitude to Guillaume Stewart for being an incredible supporter and listener, and one who inspires me to have confidence in putting my thoughts into words. And to my extended family and my network of friends, thank you all.

About the Author

Lisa R. Nelson is a graduate of Temple University. She is a senior staff member at a large non-profit family services agency in Philadelphia, where she lives. Her short stories "Thirteen" and "From Where They Sit" appeared in the anthology *From Where We Sit: Black Writers Write Black Youth*. *Drifting* is Nelson's first novel. She is currently at work on a collection of essays about black history.

From Where We Sit:
Black Writers Write Black Youth

Black Writers Write Black Youth
edited by Victoria A. Brownworth

Thirteen established and emerging African-American writers present a range of compelling and provocative stories in this exciting collection, with a wide range of dynamic characters, divergent styles, and compelling issues. Jewelle Gomez, acclaimed author of *The Gilda Stories*, offers a new episode in her historic series. Harlem native and award-winning writer Mecca Jamilah Sullivan, romance writer Anne Shade, short-story stylist Craig L. Gidney, actress and playwright Ifalade Ta'Shia Asanti, noted children's author Becky Birtha, and award-winning novelist Fiona Lewis each explore what it means to be black in America today as well as in America's historic past, addressing issues not only of race, but also of class, gender, sexual orientation, and religion. Filmmaker Lowell Boston details the multi-faceted complexities of racism in America for young black men, while emerging writers Lisa R. Nelson, Guillaume Stewart, Misty Sol, kahlil almustafa, and Quincy Scott Jones take on different aspects of urban life: Nelson presents a young girl who wants to escape her middle-class neighborhood, Stewart writes provocatively about missing fathers in black America, Sol explores the impact of gun violence and no-snitch rules, almustafa details the day-to-day suspicion young black men face, and Jones places a young black man in white academe in a dazzling display of wordplay.

ISBN 978-0-9845318-3-7

Dreaming in Color by **Fiona Lewis**

Carlene—her friends call her Cee-Cee—came to the U.S. from Jamaica to be reunited with her mother, who has been working to make enough money to send for her. But for Cee-Cee, life in her new country is hard. She misses her island home, the friends she left behind who don't even Facebook her anymore.

High school is a minefield of bullying. It's not even October and talk of homecoming and parties has Cee-Cee super depressed after the boy she likes plays an ugly trick on her. When a group of mean kids, led by one of the most popular girls in the school, targets Cee-Cee, taunting her for her accent, she turns to art as a refuge.

Then Cee-Cee meets Greg, another teen from Jamaica, who plays saxophone and has his own secrets. Greg and Cee-Cee stand up to the bullies, but then events take a devastating turn.

"Fiona Lewis grabs a handful of issues in her new novel and tosses them back out on the table with sensitivity, wisdom and clear-eyed vision. And you can't put the book down!"—Jewelle Gomez, award-winning author of The Gilda Stories

ISBN 978-0-9845318-5-1

Leave No Footprints by J.D. Shaw

It's the middle of the night when Beth Watson sneaks out of the house, steals a car, and drives, desperate to run from what she's seen, from what happened to Jack. She drives until she ends up in a sleepy little Michigan resort town as the summer season draws to a close. All Beth wants is to escape, stay unnoticed, fly under the radar. But tiny Beaumont is a town with big secrets, and Beth arrives at the same time that a murderer strikes.

Beth, who has never gone to school, never held a job, and isn't even sure if 16 is her real age, enlists the help of Dee, the town's café owner, who sees a little of herself in Beth. Beth finds herself in a world she's never known—a world of other teens, cell phones and computers, cliques and bullying, girlfriends and boyfriends. And killing. So much killing. When the murderer strikes again and again, Beth is certain her plans to start a new life are over—and the worst is yet to come.

"*Leave No Footprints* is a deftly drawn portrait of a young woman who just wants to be normal—if only she can escape her past, which is a mystery even to herself."—Joanne Dahme, author of *Tombstone Tea* and *Contagion*

ISBN 978-0-9845318-6-8

Taken Away by Patty Friedmann

It's the last week of August 2005, and Hurricane Katrina is about to hit the Gulf Coast—hard. As the storm comes closer and threatens to destroy New Orleans, 15-year-old Summer "Sumbie" Elmwood's two-year-old sister Amalia undergoes open-heart surgery. She survives the surgery, but when New Orleans is evacuated, Amalia disappears from the hospital. With the city deserted and destroyed and no food, water, electricity, or phone service available, the Elmwoods are forced to leave New Orleans without Amalia and go to Houston to stay with Sumbie's aunt. The FBI and others search for her missing sister, but thousands are missing and the little girl is no one's priority. Sumbie's parents begin to suspect that Sumbie did something to Amalia. With the aid of two would-be boyfriends, Hadyn and Robert, Sumbie tries to find her missing sister and prove her innocence in the chaos left by the killer storm. Will she succeed? Or will she become the FBI's prime suspect?

"Patty Friedmann is one of the finest writers in Louisiana. Not only did she stay in New Orleans throughout Hurricane Katrina and its aftermath, she ended up being rescued twice! No one knows New Orleans better and no one is better qualified to write about that period."—Julie Smith, Edgar Award-winning mystery author

ISBN 978-0-9845318-2-0

No Takebacks by Patty Friedmann

Otto Fisher has ADHD. He's also adopted. At thirteen, he never thought much about where he came from until his seventh-grade teacher at the prestigious St. Michael's School in New Orleans asks her class to write about an ancestor. Each student must perform their piece in a school play. Otto's adoptive mother, whom he adores, helps him write about one of her ancestors, who was in the Holocaust.

Otto's story is the most moving of all—but not for his father, a college English professor who is also a racist and an anti-Semite.

The play triggers a series of conflicts in the Fisher household, culminating in Otto's father beating his mother. Otto's older sister, Ada, stops the fight. Then their father moves out. Which leaves Otto torn between the mother and sister he adores and the father he desperately needs. When he goes to visit his father, a series of events forces everyone in the Fisher family to question the meaning of family.

In this funny, bittersweet, poignant and thoroughly engaging short novel, Otto narrates the story of his young life with humor, grace and surprising insight.

"Patty Friedmann downright tickles with her delivery, approaching serious subjects in fun, yet leaving us dazed and philosophical in the end. Like her city, New Orleans, she's ironic without the acrimony. No one does it better."—George and Wendy Rodrigue, Blue Dog series

ISBN 978-0-9849146-3-0

Immortal Longings by Diane DeKelb-Rittenhouse

Lauren and Kayla are the perfect high school couple– except they aren't actually a couple. Smart and sarcastic Lauren is secretly in love with her best friend, Kayla, one of the most popular girls at school, who changes partners (male and female) like other girls change shoes.

One autumn afternoon, the two 17-year-olds wander into Manhattan's newest vintage clothing store, Deja Nous, and agree to take after-school jobs at the enticing shop. On the ride home to Queens, Kayla talks non-stop about the wonderful clothes, how much fun she and Lauren will have working together, and the store's the intriguing and beautiful owner, Elizabeth Valiant.

Deja Nous soon becomes an obsession for the teens, but it isn't until Lauren starts putting together the puzzle pieces of the Valiant family and recent events that she realizes that she and her beloved Kayla are in danger from a centuries-old curse. Will Lauren be strong enough to save them both, or will the power of forces she never imagined be stronger than her love for Kayla?

ISBN 978-0-9845318-4-4

2012 Gold Medal Winner
Young Adult Fiction—Horror
Moonbeam Children's Book Awards